WE'RE FOREVER

AF520630

notionpress.com

WE'RE FOREVER

Paridhi Newatia

notionpress.com

Notion Press

Old No. 38, New No. 6

McNichols Road, Chetpet

Chennai - 600 031

First Published by Notion Press 2015

ISBN 978-93-5206-461-8

I want to dedicate this to – **Sanovar Lohia,** *who is as much a part of this book as i am. Everything in the publication of this book is as much hers as it is mine. From the very beginning till the very end, we've taken all steps together making our dream come true. We made it without killing each other which is such an achievement. Yes, we made our start.*

Contents

Acknowledgement

This book would not have been complete without the support of these people:

My parents, who never stopped believing that I would do it someday, Mom & Dad, thank you for everything. Pratyush whenever you said "You really writing?" motivated me so much.

Roopal, Purva, Nupur and Nidhi for dealing with my weird ideas, constantly motivating me at all hours of the day and never failing to ask me for updates.

Rohini, Ridhima, Tripti , you guys keep me sane.

Harsh, Priyo, Ayush, Additya, Siddharth, Abhimanyu and Pranav for tolerating all my loud moods and making me laugh whenever I felt low.

Akshita, Umang, Sumit, Sahil and Soumya who were perfect soundboards and always had some positive criticism for me. You were always excited for me.

Pratham Jain, for his encouragement and guidance. He had answers for all my questions.

Juhi, Priyanka and Shweta you guys always believed I could write.

Surbhi Agarwal and Sheetal Agarwal, for always telling me to keep working on it. Your smiles made me want to never give up.

Thank you for always being there guys!

1

FIRST SIGHT, FIRST FIGHT!

Beep beep. Beep beep. Beep beep…

The freaking alarm didn't stop its incessant noise. Alarm clocks should've been banned as instruments of noise pollution.

Vidisha knew the next wakeup call would be coming from her mother and that was one she could not shut up or throw against the wall.

And right there on cue, "Vidishaaa…"Her mother's voice rangthrough the door of her room. "Wake up sweetheart. It's already 9:00 and you told me you had to be at your college at 10:00."

Oh shit! She was going to be late. She could not afford to be late. She was the freaking president of the student union for crying out loud! She had a reputation to uphold!

Practically flying out of her bed, she rushed into the bathroom. "Mom, I'm really late. Could you please pack me something to eat in college?"

"Already done sweetie. I have put in your tiffin and a bottle of juice in your backpack, taken out your clothes and put your car keys by the door."

"Really? You actually did all that?" Vidisha asked, her tone conveying the disbelief she felt.

Her extremely independent mother, who had taught her to do all her own work by the time she was eight, was not a person who cleaned up after another person's(namely Vidisha's) mess.

"No! Of course I didn't! Who told you to stay out till 1 in the night when you knew you had work to do?" And then her mom went away laughing.

Vidisha groaned loudly. She really should have seen that one coming. Her mom had a wicked sense of humour which spared no one, not even her own daughter.

Her mother, Madhavi Agarwal, was her friend, confidante and conscience all rolled in one. Not just a simple housewife, she had the wisdom and that annoying, yet necessary, intuition that comes with the job description of being another. She was an interior decorator and also a columnist; her articles on decor and designing had been picked up by several local and a few national periodicals.

Dashing out, she quickly put on the first clothes she could find. Downstairs, she hopped on one foot, trying to put on her shoes and at the same time almost inhaling some toast with a glass of juice.

She almost got arrested in her hurry to reach college, jumping several red lights & speeding to pretty dangerous limits. But, she made it to college well on time, being just 10 minutes late.

She got out and checked her cell.17 missed calls out of which 11 were from her friend Reva, who also happened to be in charge of the budget allotted for the fest. Oh, and did she mention that she was the President of the student union.

That meant she was in charge of the whole freaking affair which was already proving to be a major pain in the ass.

Hurrying across the parking lot, she strode to the room which had been converted into the main office for the fest. At that moment she had a million and one things to do and she had to do them NOW!

A little ahead she heard a little commotion. One of the voices was a little familiar. Vidisha gave another moan. That voice belonged to Reva Narayan, trouble shooter and cyber whiz extraordinaire.

Reva was a 5'2" firecracker who looked like an angel but had probably sold her soul to the devil before she could speak coherently. Fiercely loyal, she was a mad psycho genius, not to mention that half of Vidisha's troubles could be laid at her doorstep. Currently she was on the verge of bitch slapping a group of giggling, very dense first years.

"You DO NOT play dress up with the drama costumes! They are not for your amusement. It is for those actors who are going to get the college the drama trophy for the third year in a row, not a bunch of blonde bimbos who have lipstick for brains!" Reva screamed at the top of her lungs.

This year the Shakespeare Club, the drama department at St.Lawrence College had a new kid for the costumes. Apparently, he could create runway standard magic with any piece of fabric and a pair of scissors. So this time the costumes were out of the world beautiful and a number of attempts to steal them had already been made, mostly by a few dumb girls who would otherwise have never had the chance to wear such gorgeous gowns anyway.

Unfortunately for them, they were too dumb to pull it off and with Reva's hawkish eyes hovering over all assets, not one single outfit was filched.

"VIDISHA AGARWAL! Where the hell have you been? Do you have any idea of the amount of paper work which needs your fucking approval?" Without waiting for an answer she continued, "No of course you don't! Because her highness has to have her 10 hours of beauty sleep."

Damn! Reva had a tendency to pour out her ire on any creature unfortunate enough to cross her way. However, she was right and Vidisha did need to get into her work. So Vidisha humbly listened to her tirade and made appropriate apologetic noises. When it felt that Reva was calm enough, she went to her desk to tackle the much dreaded paperwork.

Three gruelling hours later...

Vidisha finally took a breather from the backbreaking monstrosity of addressing the formal invitations which had to be sent to the VIPs.

She had also supervised (read: screamed, threatened, hauled and blackmailed) the moving of the crates of drinks and food for the catering dept for a good hour. Before that, she physically coerced a group of lazy juniors to help the design team in decorating the college auditorium where most of the indoors events would take place. Right now she was hungry, thirsty, tired and basically at the end of her tether.

She was just adding the final touches on a poster, advertising the fest, when a shadow fell on it.

"Excuse me? Could you please tell me the dates for the dance competition and photography exhibition?" A deep, husky voice, like rough silk, caressed her ears. She looked up, and up, into warm, beautiful brown eyes several shades lighter than her own black ones.

Those eyes belonged to a face that generally graced magazine centrefolds. Sharp eyebrows, a long aquiline nose and the hard set of his jaw gave him a serious appearance. This seriousness was only tempered by his expression which looked as if he had just heard the world's most amusing joke. A soft smile played around his lips and Vidisha felt like joining in his obvious delight, whatever it may be.

However, her mind was bogged down by the massive work load of the fest. She was barely able to register the guy's hotness quotient and for a second Vidisha was lost. She could see his lips moving and had to drag herself forcibly out of the haze of lust and tiredness that engulfed her.

"…from SLM college. I wanted to know the final dates for the entry?" the guy said.

"By the way my name is Varun Choudhary"

Vidisha just kept looking at him.

"Ummm…are you listening?" He asked. Then he casually waved a hand in front of her face. "Or do I need a bull horn and visual representation? He added with a laugh.

And Vidisha's tired brain snapped. And sadly, it went straight to psychotic bitch mode.

"Excuse me! Are you implying that I am retarded? Or that I am physically impaired?

"Wait…what? No, no, no, no, no. I didn't mean anything of that sort." He stammered. The look of worry and astonishment on his face was just too adorable.

"Of course you didn't, because you have all the time in the world to waste and who better to waste it with than li'l ol' me, isn't it?" She added sarcastically.

"Ok, now I am seriously considering mental deficiency as an option. I did not mean to insult you; I was simply making a joke. You looked kind of tired and I just thought...."

"Oh you thought, did you? What did you think? Oh look! A dumb girl whom I can flirt with and who knows she might just be the mother of my imaginary children." Well you've got some balls dude. Do you think I am running a charity here? I have serious work to do and you are simply being a menace. Now get your stupid ass off my college and don't show me your face ever again!"

There was a moment of stunned silence, where you could hear even the softest whisper. Vidisha was aware that a few people had gathered around to witness the heated exchange.

As for the guy, he stood stunned as if he had been told that she ate puppies for breakfast. Soon the shocked look gave way to anger and he gave as well as he got.

"What the hell! I am a participant in your stupid fest to which my college was invited. I have absolutely no interest in hitting on a girl like you...."

Uh-oh. Vidisha realised that she had hit a nerve. Her bitchy state could be attributed to frazzled nerves. Looks like she would have to apologise but wait a second... "What do you mean by a girl like me?"

"... I'm not done. I was nothing less than absolutely polite. And as I am a visitor, you should have been equally polite and even more courteous. But no, you are stuck up, snobbish, rude and pretty much an uptight bitch. Geez, you really need to loosen up and get a life, girl."

"That's it!" She thought. The thin tether she had on her temper snapped.

"Who the HELL do you think you are?!! Just because you've got pretty eyes does not mean you can say whatever shit erupts in your mind. I have a crap load of work to do and you are a fucking waste of my time and energy. And in case you thought I wasn't paying attention to what you said if you want to know the dates for the events and timing just look at the fucking bulletin board outside. That's what those things are for."

"Listen lady! I am an outsider wanting to participate in your bloody fest. You were the first person I saw, which is why I asked for directions. But YOU, you are the most uptight bitch I have ever had the misfortune to come across. Screw you and your fest. Go to HELL!!

Vidisha stared at him blankly as the guy pivoted and stormed away. For a moment she felt some slight pangs of guilt but she immediately squashed it away and concentrated on her task.

She had a kick-ass fest to prepare for.

2

RAINBOW NIGHTS

The pulsating beats of Koop Island Blues permeated into Vidisha's soul. She felt herself drowning in a pleasant haze of alcohol and the utter contentment of a job well done. The past week had been a strain, not only on her but all those involved in organising the fest. The fest had glossed over without a hitch. All the events had gone smoothly. Her college had won most of the trophies, including the much coveted Overall Performer's trophy. This meant that her dean would be very pleased with her. And the budget which she wanted approved for the upcoming class trip would be ensured.

Slightly tipsy, she walked up to the stage and like a queen observing her realm, cast an indulgent gaze over the hundreds of students lost to the joy of the beat of the music. She had already had two beers and somebody had just thrust another one in her hands. She saw a group of her friends dancing near the edge of the grounds and climbed down the stairs to join them. Although she was wearing a thigh high dress, she could not feel the cold. As she was walking down, her 4 inch heels were not much of a help to her. Staggering slightly, she worked her way into the crowd of writhing bodies and was immediately engulfed by them. Once again she gave herself up to the music.

She did not need anyone. She was dancing all by herself and was happy in her own little world. Suddenly a pair of rough hands grabbed her and she was spun around roughly. A tall beefy guy (she recognised him as a participant from another college) whose breath reeked of alcohol was pawing her like some desperate animal.

"Get off of me, you ugly dog!" she said while she tried to push him away.

"Oh, come on, pretty girl. You know you want me."

"No, you pig."

"Those moves you got say something entirely different." He said, all the while keeping a strong grip on her forearms.

Vidisha saw red. If there was one thing she hated was being hit upon by the dumbest of guys. Thank God for her ultra-ambitious mother who had insisted that she join tae - kwon - do classes at the age of twelve. This time she would be using a very basic, universal move. Lightly grasping the wrist of the guy who was holding her, she angled herself and kneed him swiftly in the balls. The guy let out a howling roar of pain and dropped to his knees in front of her.

"Listen to me carefully, because what I'm saying applies for all women. One, do not touch me without my permission. And two, when I say 'No', I mean 'No'." She flattened him to the ground with a vicious kick to his shin.

She was just about to punch him in the face when another pair of arms grabbed her from behind and pulled her away from the pervert who was whimpering like a baby. She struggled against the other person who was holding her and giving them a violent shove she managed to push the other person away.

Unfortunately, the momentum caused her to trip on her heels. Before she could hit the hard ground, those arms caught her and steadied her. Slightly shaken she took two deep breathes and calmed down a little. She was able to register a few things now. One, this new pair of arms was not touching her inappropriately. And second, this other guy had physically lifted her away and was taking her God knows where. She started to panic but the other guy said, "Calm down. I'm just taking you to the cafeteria. You need some cold water." Gradually Vidisha stopped struggling. This guy was helping her and she thought she had heard his voice before.

He put her down gently and said, "Geez, aren't you a little wild cat?"

Vidisha's temper flared again. She looked up and saw the guy, his features half-hidden in the dark. She could not see him clearly. But it was obvious it was not someone she knew. She felt a vague sense that she had met him before, but she tamped it down and got a grip on herself. Then it registered; he was the guy she had shouted upon the other day. Talk about embarrassing.

"I'm fine. I'm fine." She steadied herself. She was aware that she looked like a mess right now.

They moved together to the cafeteria. The college cafe was a beautiful building located at one end of the campus. It was the favourite haunt for most of the student population. Because it was the time of the fest, several campus buildings, including the cafe, had been locked down. However, a small storeroom had been kept open with basic supplies for the over-nightie's and the residing faculties.

'The other guy' (what was his name? Vidisha was struggling to remember it) made her sit down on one of the benches which lined the lawn outside the café and went to get her a bottle of water. In the meantime, Vidisha fished out her cell and updated Reva about her situation. She told her not to worry and to go home if she wanted to. Vidisha was not worried about herself; she had her car after all.

Hearing footsteps, she looked up to see 'the other guy', as she had dubbed her mysterious saviour, coming up to her. He had a bottle of chilled water and a packet of chips in his hands. Although she didn't say anything, her stomach was grateful to him.

The buildings might have been deserted but the entire campus was lit with soft lights, giving it an otherworldly feel. 'The other guy' handed her the water and proceeded to open the chips. All the while he had a smile on his face, and if she wasn't mistaken, a look of pride. Well, he would have to join the line. Vidisha was pretty proud of herself too. Never had she thought that kicking a man in the jewels would feel so good; definitely calling for a mental pack on the back.

"That was a damn good kick there. I thought about helping you out when I first saw you guys, but by the time I reached there you had the scene quite under control." He said, all the while smiling in that sexy way.

"I sure did. By the way, I did not thank you for helping me out." Vidisha held out her hand for him to shake. "I'm Vidisha."

"I'm Varun. And Vidisha, it wasn't you I was helping out. That poor guy whimpering on the ground was the one I was saving. And since you were the lighter option, it was you I chose to carry away." All this he said with bright twinkle in his eyes.

Vidisha couldn't help but admire his wit. She gave him a grin of her own and took a long swig of the water.

He sat down beside her and half reclined on the bench. Vidisha freed her feet from the prison of her heels and after a whole week, allowed herself to relax. Crossing her legs, she rested her neck on the back of the bench. The night-sky was plush with diamonds, winking and twinkling. Both of them sat together sat in companionable silence, swapping mindless, entertaining tales now and then. Slowly the silence faded away and a steady flow of conversation rooted in true warmth came forth. They found that they had many mutual friends and to each other's surprise were in the same school for around a year. Tales were swapped, laughter shared and memories enjoyed.

At one point she suggested half-heartedly that they return to the party but they simultaneously dismissed the idea. Vidisha had the outrageous idea to loot the caretaker's secret stash of booze and Varun immediately agreed to be her partner in crime.

They tiptoed to one of the small sheds used by the college staff. Because Vidisha was the council President, she had a really good knowledge of the various quirks of the various members of the staff. This particular guy, Ghanshyam bhaiya, was a notorious bribe taker. Some of her classmates had bribed him to help smuggle their booze into the college and Vidisha knew for a fact that the guy hid his ill-fetched earnings in this very shed. Putting Varun in charge of looking out for unwanted visitors, she entered the shed and moved to the pile of unused cartons at the end of it. Rummaging in them, she finally hit jackpot; a bottle of Smirnoff.

They ran away from the shed and went to the lawn again. Passing the booze between them, they talked the night away. Vidisha was now under a pleasant buzz and she felt liberated as never before. Awesome would have been the perfect way to describe her now. And the company was not bad either.

She was now very aware of Varun. He had beautiful brown eyes. She took in the tiny details which had escaped her the other day. He was pretty tall too. Even in her heels he must have topped her by a good 5 inches, putting him well above 6 feet. He also had the sexiest laugh she had ever heard. She was very, very comfortable with him and Vidisha realised one thing: she did not want this night to end.

By this time, the alcohol was definitely affecting her. She was holding her heels and the grass was tickling her bare feet. The bottle of vodka was almost empty and she had no recollection of when that happened. Suddenly, she stumbled along the path and Varun steadied her with an arm around her waist. Vidisha put her hands on his chest and was taken aback a little at how close he was to her. They were now close enough to the party to be able to hear the music but were hidden by a lush canopy of trees so they could not be seen or overheard. The strains of Atif Aslam's 'Gulabi Ankhen' could be heard over the huge speakers. Varun's hand tightened and he pulled her closer to him. Vidisha should have been afraid or nervous but for the first time in her life, she felt a soul-deep connection with someone. Holding her close, Varun moved them in time to the music; all the while they did not take their eyes from each other. The world reduced to a kaleidoscope of colours and sensations. A night drenched in magic, in hope.

Vidisha focused on reality and was startled to see that had they moved even an inch closer, their lips would have been touching. She quickly moved out of his warm embrace and the guy too jumped back as if on hot coals. They cleared their throats and tried not to look as guilty as they felt.

"I think that we should get back. Reva might be getting worried."

"I think so too."

The brief bubble of intimacy had been shattered. The easiness between the two was now underscored by awkwardness.

"Bye Varun. And, umm, thanks again, for everything."

"I hope I'll see you again."

As Vidisha walked back to the lights, she turned around just once to look at him. He was walking away the other way. Vidisha stopped and looked at him until he was swallowed by the darkness. Then Vidisha allowed herself to be absorbed into the spectrum of light behind her.

3

IN VINO VERITAS

The next day, Vidisha woke up to a raging headache. She had a vague sense of nausea and the dim sunlight which had somehow managed to slip through a few cracks in the curtains, blinded her already sensitive eyes. She really should not have had that last round of shots. Somehow managing to lift herself from her pillow, she rummaged through her bedside drawer for her handy Aspirin. Popping two pills, she downed them with an entire glass of water. After that, she again plopped down on the bed and thought about the night before.

She could not help the satisfactory grin that crept on her face, nor could she control the giggle as she recalled the pervert's face when he sank to his knees. Why were guys so infinitely stupid? But, not all of them were like that. There were good guys too. Good Samaritans who came to your help if they thought you required it. Guys like Varun. Vidisha was aware that last night was a series of firsts. Dancing under the moonlight with a heart-breakingly gorgeous guy definitely made the cut.

Her cell phone beeped to show a new image sent by Reva. Damn! She had not wanted to meet anyone after last night's fiasco. So she had sent Reva a text telling her to go home. Vidisha knew she was acting weird, she also knew that eventually she would have to explain things. Vidisha opened her Whatsapp and a large smile spread on her face. Reva had sent her a selfie with her and one of their closest friends, Saket. Beneath the picture it was written:

"Guess who is back from the wild?"

She immediately typed back:

'5:30 today? Usual *adda*?'

Reva sent her two thumbs-ups as a reply.

Vidisha fell back on the pillows, happy after a long, long time. Too much time had passed since she had seen Saket. She reclined back in the bed, wondering if she could sleep for a few more moments. A glimpse at the clock showed her that it was one in the afternoon. Fuck fuck fuckitty fuck! Thanking the heavens and all the thirty-three million Hindu deities for her laid back parents, she dragged herself out of her bed and literally crawled into the bathroom. Ten minutes later, she emerged feeling much fresher and clear-headed. Her stomach growled with hunger and she headed downstairs for some breakfast. Oh wait! That would be lunch now.

As she reached the kitchen, the front door opened and her father came in for lunch. On seeing her, he gave a huge smile. She was the apple of his eye. Her mom too came out of her home-office and for a second the trio stared blankly at each other. They burst out laughing at the absurdity of the moment. While her mom went into the kitchen to prepare lunch, Vidisha and her dad sat down at the dining table.

"How was your fest, *beta*? You came home quite late last night so we couldn't ask you then and your mother refused to let me wake you up this morning…"

"Obviously! She has been working non-stop from the past one month, juggling college, work and that fest. She deserves a break." Her mom said from the kitchen.

Vidisha smiled as she poured a glass of juice for her and her father. No matter how strict her parents were at times, they never passed on a chance to pamper her if need be.

"*Beta*, I've been meaning to ask you, have you decided to talk to Sangeeta about the Raheja baby shower?" Her dad asked.

Sangeeta Kabra was an old family friend of the Agarwals. She was the Founder and Managing Director of a major event management company in Kolkata and catered to the needs of many clients in Ranchi too. She had long noticed Vidisha's flair for design and tasteful organisation and had given her an internship in her Ranchi branch. Not only did it look good in her resume, Vidisha actually enjoyed her work. She loved meeting new people and she desperately wanted to build contacts and get good references for her company applications.

She had now been working for 'Starstruck' for a year and a half, and she already had an impressive number of successful events to add to her CV. Indeed there were now times when she was in charge of many minor events such as bachelor/bachelorette parties, small corporate events, kids' birthdays, theme inspired cocktail lunches and so on. Major events such as weddings were also part of her job profile, but she was usually a part of a large team then.

The Raheja baby shower would have been quite a coup de grace; the only problem was that the mother-in-law of the new mom was the modern equivalent of a fire-breathing dragon. Prone to throwing hissy fits of epic proportions, Mrs Mina Raheja had managed to piss off every single 'Starstruck' employee single-handedly. Hell, she made rabid dogs look like fluffy rabbits. Vidisha still shuddered at some of the tantrums she had witnessed:

On deciding the colour scheme for the shower, "This shade of pink is not pink enough. I wanted blush and this is more rose. Are you people colour-blind?!"

At the menu tasting, "The food is not classy enough!! And who put in Indian for the cuisine? The menu has to have at least five different international cuisines." (As if food is supposed to be classy?? Give me tasty Indian food any day and I'll be content for life)

At one time she had hit a poor intern with her purse just because she hadn't liked the party favours he had proposed.

So basically, everyone was either scared shitless or pissed off beyond measure. At the last brainstorming session one of the junior assistants, Mahi had finally lost it and had threatened to quit if she had to deal with the 'sadistic bitch' (her words) again. By the time she had finished convincing her, several others too had raised protests. The end result of it was that Vidisha was chosen to take up the matter with Sangeeta ma'am and explain to her the entire situation. She had already been informed about it over the phone but she was coming to Ranchi within the week to get a feel of things. But, by that time she was supposed to hold the fort and appease the sadistic bitch's every whim.

The only thing stopping Vidisha from completely giving up the project was Neha, the new mom of the cutest baby girl. She was the complete opposite of her mother-in-law and was a perfect sweetheart. The baby shower was her idea, her dream, but Mina had taken over and become such a raging bitch that even Hitler would have cowered before her. Vidisha sincerely hoped that Sangeeta would salvage the problem before it got out of hand.

"Yeah Dad. I talked to her two days back and she said to handle the situation till she arrives." Vidisha came to the present and focused on her dad.

"Ugh! That Mina Raheja is one evil woman." Her mom said from the kitchen, "I sometimes pity poor Neha. That poor girl has to deal with that monster on a daily basis. As a matter of fact, the last time I met her in the club she was chewing off the head of a poor waiter for messing up her order."

Vidisha went into the kitchen to help her mom bring out the food. Despite the myriad of issues hovering over her, her mind was still with a gorgeous brown-eyed boy with whom she had danced.

"Mom, I'll be going out in the evening today. It's 'Us Time'."

Her mom gave her a suspicious look and for a second Vidisha felt guilty. But her entire family knew not to bother if it was 'Us Time'.

They sat down together and Vidisha scarfed down toast, *poha* and fruits as if she was starving. The rumbling in her tummy calmed down and Vidisha was able to pay more attention to her parents' conversation.

She gave a soft smile when she noticed that her parents were completely engrossed in each other. Although theirs was an arranged marriage, the love that literally overflowed between the two of them never failed to touch her heart. Even after almost twenty-five years of marriage, they were as giddy as teenagers. Vidisha honestly hoped that one day she too would find such a fulfilling love.

Within minutes she finished her late brunch. She got up from the table and putting her plate in the sink, she quietly went up to her room. Her parents were not even aware that she had left. For a moment, she was tempted to tease them out of their lovey-dovey bubble, but a quick glance at the clock told her that her little brother would be doing it in approximately fifteen minutes when he would be arriving from school.

Entering her room, she worked up a minor panic on seeing its dishevelled state. Being the obsessive-compulsive freak that she was, last night's mess was like a red flag to her. The gorgeous coral dress she had worn last night was lying rumpled on the floor, one of her shoes was hanging from the wardrobe handle by its strap and its twin was nowhere to be seen. Her vanity was overflowing with all sorts of hair and make-up products. The bed was unmade and there was a rainbow of pillows scattered all over the floor. Overall, it looked like a bomb had been detonated in her room.

Vidisha gave a mental groan and went to tackle the pig-sty that was her room.

Two and a half hours later…

It was 4:30 and Vidisha had half an hour to get ready and reach her destination. Her room was looking much better now and she already felt more at peace with herself. She just had time for a quick shower before she would head out.

When she came out of the bathroom, she put on her most comfortable and most tattered pair of cut-offs and adding an equally comfortable loose cotton T-shirt, she was almost ready to go. She didn't bother to brush her unruly hair and just about managed to contain it a loose ponytail.

Downstairs, she took her keys and called out to her mom that she would be going out to meet the 'gang'. 'Gang' was probably an over-rated term for her and her two best friends, but that was that they had always called themselves. Hell, their parents all agreed that the three of them together caused more mayhem than a bunch of rabid monkeys jacked up on crack.

Saket, Reva and Vidisha. The Three Musketeers. The bane of the entire neighbourhood and the reason behind all of Verma Aunty's broken windows.

They had more or less grown up together and their families being close too were more like siblings rather than just friends. Apart from her parents, they were the only people Vidisha truly trusted. Right now they were meeting at their usual spot, Heera's Chai Dukan.

Ten years ago, what started as a roadside stall was now a little better in the sense that Heera bhaiya, the owner had added a few tables and chairs and added a number of dishes to his regular menu. It was a mere ten minutes from Vidisha's place, located near the Morabadi grounds. Although the hygiene was still questionable, there was no denying that the tea and Maggi served there were beyond compare. The three of them had been going there for as long as Vidisha could remember. They even had their own table fixed now, not to mention, the entire staff knew them.

She parked her car and went to wait at their regular table. She knew that she would have to explain to Reva what had actually happened last night, and in a way she wanted some guy advice too, and who better than her two best friends? Saket and Reva would be coming together because they lived in the same apartment building. But because they lived farther away, it would take them a little time to reach there; which was good, as it gave Vidisha time to compose herself and garner her thoughts coherently.

What was she going to do? What was she actually doing?? She had absolutely no clue whatsoever. God! She was turning into a crazy chick who was getting obsessed over a guy who she knew nothing about.

No, dammit, no! She had to think of something else.

Taking a deep breath, she forced herself to focus on meeting Saket after so many months. He was home after so long. The last time she had seen him had been in Holi. As an intern at one of India's leading news stations, he barely had time to breathe, let alone lay back and spend time with his friends and family.

He had been living in Delhi from the past three years and had just finished his journalism course this year. Shy and serious, he was the perfect package; the loving son, the loyal friend and the obedient student. This was probably why he had immediately landed his internship at Khabar India. His aim in life was to be a crack investigative journalist.

Losing his grandfather at the tender age of seven to a bank robbery gone wrong had made him keenly aware of a mediocre infrastructure and the fickle-mindedness of the authorities, especially the police.

One day he came home to find out that a reporter had managed to infiltrate and expose a gang of crooks who were responsible for a number of bank robberies. This also happened to be the very gang that had shot his innocent grandfather in broad daylight. The reporter was applauded for his brave efforts and that very day, Saket vowed to himself to be like that reporter and never let anyone lose a part of their family again.

Although this childhood incident was the driving force of his hopes and dreams, Saket never let this tragedy affect him negatively. Hell, he grew up to be a better person than most people. Mature, dedicated and intelligent, Vidhi always felt herself fortunate that she was a part of his life. However, serious does not equate dull or boring. Saket was a guy who partied hard and worked harder. You could talk to him about anything under the sun and he was never short of sane, reasonable advice. Advice that Vidisha generally listened to (he did give pretty good advice) and which Reva as a rule, chose to shoot down.

Speaking of whom, Reva was, like, Saket's polar opposite. Wild, unruly, a total madcap. She could talk a mile a minute, instil the fear of God in anyone dumb enough to cross her and hatched outrageously elaborate schemes guaranteed to get Vidisha in trouble. She was an IT student in the same college as Vidisha. True to her psychotic form, she wanted to be a hacker. The only saving grace was that she wanted to be an 'ethical hacker' and work *against* cybercrime. Vidisha had no doubt she would succeed. Reva was like a dog with a bone. Once she set her sights on something, she never let go.

Sometimes Vidisha felt a little inadequate in front of her friends. Both of them had such grand dreams of achieving something meaningful with their lives. Their dreams could get better lives for people. She remembered the day she opened up to her mom about it…

It was around a year ago.

Saket had just graduated from college and had gotten his much coveted internship. Reva too had gone to Delhi to attend a summer course on .NET and DBSM programming. Vidisha was missing them like hell and was moping around the house like a lost puppy. Her mom had picked up on her crappy mood, fixed two steaming mugs of coffee and had made her spill out her heart.

"Mom," Vidisha had said, "they are doing good, real good. But what am I doing? Sometimes it feels like I am just playing at make-believe and dress up."

The next words her mom had said had changed Vidisha's entire mind-set forever…

"Darling, I love Saket and Reva as much as I do you, but, they are different people, their own persons. None of you can be the same. I have always believed that human beings come on this earth to bring joy to others. You came and brought great joy for me and your dad. The same goes for them. I believe that they will bring joy to others too, through the paths that they will choose. You, sweetheart, will also do just that, albeit in a different way. You bring joy to all those people for whom you make their special day

even more memorable. Those bags you design, they are necessities that I am sure women will one day kill to buy. The happiness you give to a bride on her wedding day, creating the dream she always wanted, that satisfaction the office-worker feels when his clients are impressed by the product launch, they are all something meaningful which you have done; and I am very, very proud of you, both me and your dad."

A smile played on Vidisha's lips as she relived that particular memory. After that day she had never looked back. Any lingering doubts she had had completely evaporated and she threw herself into her work with renewed vigour. It was then that Sangeeta had started noticing her and she had started getting better and larger assignments.

The sudden revving of a two-wheeler brought her out of her reverie and she looked up to see her two closest friends grinning at her like crazy. Reva was driving her hot pink scooty and Saket looked as if he had been dragged through the seven circles of hell. Vidisha could sympathize with him; on her best days Reva barely got through by narrowly avoiding at least ten innocent pedestrians. Not to mention that she usually drove like a newly escaped bat from hell.

Parking the scooty, Saket and Reva joined Vidisha at their usual table. Immediately, Mohan, Heera's son brought their standard order of masala chai and Maggi. He was a young boy of sixteen and wanted to become an engineer. He had already passed his boards with flying colours and had managed to snag a scholarship at one of Ranchi's top schools. He worked in the evenings at his father's shop and many a times Vidisha and her friends had helped him out by lending him their old books, copies and any other stuff which they felt would have helped him.

Saket gave Vidisha a long warm hug. It was his sweet wordless way of expressing how much he had missed her. Seeing her two closest friends together put her in a state of calm.

"So, why were you out playing Mr India last night?" Reva asked.

"Huh?"

"You were MIA the entire time last night, and when I called you, you sent me a cryptic message to go home. So what really happened babes?"

Both Saket and Reva turned questioning gazes at her.

For a second Vidisha was unsure. What would she say to them, 'Last night I kicked a guy in the balls, stole a bottle of vodka, danced with a stranger under the moonlight and that happens to be the high point of my life till date?'

Yeah, she didn't think that would go down well with them. She decided to opt for a softer approach, "I kind of met someone last night." She blurted out abruptly.

Well that got their attention. Two shocked pair of eyes stared back at her.

"Come again now??"

"It just happened. I don't know who he was, actually what happened was some pervert came on to me last night and pissed me off so I ended up kicking him where it really hurts and I was about to do some more damage when this guy literally pulled me off of him. Then, because I was still in a very shitty mood we didn't go back to the party instead we sat near the canteen and from where we filched some of the caretaker's stock…"

"Hold on a second. Did you just say you stole from asshole Ghanshyam'ssuper-secret stock of alcohol?" Reva interjected with a huge grin on her face.

"Yeaaaaah…it's really not that secret, you know." Vidisha grinned back at her.

"And then as I was saying…it was me, the guy and a glorious bottle of White Mischief. I obviously don't need to tell you guys how drunk I got, but let's just say it was pretty awesome. We talked for hours about everything and anything and it felt good to open up to a perfect stranger but the damn climax was when we were coming back to the party. 'Gulabi Ankhen' was playing and the guy just grabbed me and we sort of kind of, danced to it, under the night sky. Damn that was sexy. !"

Her story was met by lots of cheering and a bunch of wolf whistles (by Reva of course). Both her friends were grinning like maniacs.

"Girl, I am so glad for you. It was high time you got some." Saket said.

Vidisha also joined in their laughter; it felt good to be able to meet up her friends like this. The rest few hours passed away in a whirl of Maggi, coffee and warm memories.

As they were leaving Reva asked Vidisha, "Hey what happened to the guy, whose balls you kicked?" Vidisha answered with an evil grin, 'The last time I checked, he had his friends searching for an ice pack for his crotch."

4

NETIZEN

There was a continuing tradition in Varun's house that his father would wake him up via text. His father strongly believed that today's generation was more responsive to electronic media than actual human interaction. He may not like it, but even he agreed that it was a better alternative to repeating the same thing over and over without a response.

This morning Varun woke up to a promise of coffee waiting for him. He sent a swift reply to his dad, keeping it concise.

'I'm awake. See you in 5, Dad.'

Fifteen minutes later, Varun was sitting down with his parents and enjoying the pleasant morning.

"How did the fest go, beta?" his mother asked.

"It went great, Maa. Our college did really well. And the finale last night was exceptionally memorable." Varun couldn't help the smile on his face. He continued, "As a matter of fact, I have to go there again to make sure we get the correct number of certificates."

"Won't they send it to your college directly?" his mom asked.

"Umm, yeah. But I, uh, I have to take care of some details, and, oh yeah, I'll meet up with Piyush too." Varun hastily made up the excuse. Thankfully his mom seemed to buy it so he gave a huge sigh of relief.

The chief reason he was jumping to go to St. Lawrence was just so he could catch a glimpse of Vidisha again. As much as he tried to deny it, he was definitely intrigued by her. Piyush and the certificates were mere excuses.

He knew that Piyush didn't have any official classes today and called him up.

"Hey man. What plans for today?"

"Nothing *yaar*, just wrapping up some fest work. I'll be free in an hour or so. You want to meet up?

"Sure dude. See you then."

Two hours later Varun was inside St. Lawrence, slightly pissed off at his friend. He had been waiting since the past hour and there was no hair or hide of Piyush. He tried his cell for the umpteenth time and finally Piyush picked up.

"Where the hell are you? I've been waiting since the past hour and trying your goddamned cell like a million times!"

"*Yaar*, I'm so sorry. One of the professors' in-charge stopped us and was going on about some shit or other. Anyways, where are you, man? I'm on the way."

"I'm near the parking lot. Be quick."

Varun hung up and subconsciously looked around, his gaze searching something, or someone.

A few minutes later he saw Piyush coming to him, his entire demeanour harangued.

"Thanks man. That teacher was really irritating us. I just barely managed to get away. Come on, let's go to the canteen. I really need a drink."

On their way to the canteen, Piyush kept up a running diatribe about the fest. The response they had received was overwhelming. Plus the college had got some seriously impressive PR. Even Varun had been impressed by the quality with which the fest had been conducted.

They had just arrived at the canteen when a voice that Varun knew he would never forget interrupted them.

"Piyush! Piyush, wait up."

They turned around to see Vidisha running up to them. At first she was only looking at Piyush, her eyes sliding right past Varun. She did a double-take and looked back at him. The hesitant smile she gave him did something funny to him.

"You're the guy who helped me out yesterday. Varun, right?"

To meet such a charming girl two times in a row felt too good to be true, but Varun was not about to question his luck. If he were to be honest, he had been hoping to maybe catch a glimpse of her. But to actually meet her was a far shot. Right now she was looking at him with a warm open demeanour and Varun couldn't help getting to know her better.

"It's you! From last night! Thanks once again. I had great fun last night"

"It was no big deal. You shouldn't have been subjected to that shithead."

Vidisha laughed and talked to Piyush for a few minutes. Meanwhile, Varun was desperately racking his brains for a way to prolong their conversation. He could see that she would go if they had nothing to say to her, "Umm, yeah! Vidisha? Could you tell me when we would be getting the trophies for the events we won in the fest"

Varun felt like banging his head on the nearest wall.

Talk about dumb questions! Piyush and Vidisha were looking a little confused and he hastened to wade his way through the shit he had spread.

"Never mind. I'm sure you've got it covered. Anyways umm, Piyush and I are going to the canteen. Would you like to join us?"

"I would have loved to, but I can't. I have some important work to do. You guys enjoy. Bye."

She turned around and went away, not realising that a certain boy with a beautiful smile was still staring at her.

Varun has a hard time taking his eyes off Vidisha's retreating back. He only tore away his gaze when Piyush gave him a particular vicious slap upside his head.

"Dude! What the fuck are you staring at?"

"Shit! Nothing man. You didn't have to hit me like that."

"You were staring at her like you wanted to eat her up. I'm warning you. Don't get any ideas about Vidisha. She's way hot and way out of your league."

Varun was absently rubbing his head and still gazing in the direction she had gone.

"Yeah. She really is damn hot."

(Few days later)

At around seven in the evening both men were lounging in Piyush's room, surfing the net and having Maggie. Piyush was getting them something to drink and Varun was checking his mail. Piyush's mom and younger brother were out, so it was just them. As he was lying on the bed with the laptop on his stomach, he felt his cell buzzing on the nightstand so he reached out for it. Bringing it to him, he realised that it was not his but rather Piyush's cell phone. However, he felt a jolt of surprise when he saw that Piyush had received a Facebook message from Vidisha Agarwal. As he put down Piyush's cell an idea came to him. Piyush had a personal laptop which he kept connected to the net whenever possible. Piyush also happened to be a Facebook addict and was pretty much online 24*7. Varun quickly opened Piyush's browser to his Facebook page and pumped his fists in the air when he saw that Piyush was tagged in.

He tamped down the slight tings of guilt and typed in search of Vidisha Agarwal.

"Dude! What the hell are you doing?" Varun jumped a mile from the bed and shifted the laptop so that Piyush couldn't see it. He mentally slapped himself that he was so engrossed that he didn't even realize his friend entering.

"Man you're so screwed" Piyush scoffed at him. You are going to net stalk her now?"

"Fuck off!" Varun pushed Piyush away and continued to browse through Vidisha's profile. Piyush gave an exasperated sigh and left him to his devises.

Ten minutes later Varun had sent Vidisha a friend request from his account and was wearing what Piyush calls a 'shit-eating' grin.

That grin became even wider when he received a notification that Vidisha Agarwal had accepted his friend request.

5

SIX DEGREES OF SEPARATION

Misusing your friend's phone is one's birth right. If your luck is good, there comes a time when your friend may leave his phone with you unattended and of course, as his friend it is your utmost duty to extract the maximum amount of data you can.

Feeling content and quite a bit proud of him, Varun went back to lying on the bed. Piyush wasn't back yet and Varun began to go through his call. He tapped on the gallery icon and started clicking random pictures. The third one he tapped turned out to one where Piyush was taking a selfie with a bunch of people. But the highlight was the image of a certain black-eyed beauty with a bewitching smile that caught Varun's attention. Damn, all his life he had gone without even knowing the existence of this girl and now it seemed as if he couldn't even go a day without seeing her or thinking about her or hearing someone else talk about her. Damn!

Whatever, Varun had tried going down that road once, you know, the whole relationship, serious commitment thing and that had gone up in flames. At one point, literally, when his ex-had attempted to burn a few of his things to just piss him off. Things had taken a turn into funny land when the pile just wouldn't burn and his ex-kept on wasting match after match. Finally, fed up with the entire scenario, Varun had to bodily remove her from his house (yes, she had the balls to develop her arson skills in his house) and clean her mess before his parents arrived and gave him the third degree.

Vidisha sure as hell was hot, but no way was Varun going beyond that.

Vidisha was running late, again. This had been happening far too often nowadays and it was now starting to annoy her. Today she was late for her friends, Aarav's, home coming party. After three years of living in London, he had returned to India for his sister's wedding. In honour of his return, a few of his old friends had thrown a huge-ass party for him at one of Ranchi's Hotels. From the looks of it, anyone who was anyone had been invited. Vidisha had been in the same class as Aarav's and had been extremely pleased to hear from him. There was no way she was missing out on meeting him, no matter how brief it would be.

Right now, she was on the way to pick up Reva, and a few of their other friends before going, to the party. And because she was a 'little' late (ok fine, she was a lot late!)

her friends were throwing a major tantrum. She stepped on the gas as she heard her cell ring for the sixth time.

On arriving at the hotel where the party was held, Varun left out a huge groan. There was a line of cars a fucking mile long! It would take him 15 minutes just to get to the valet. Why the hell had he let his friend talk him into coming, he didn't know. He knew Aarav because he was the son of his father's friend and he liked him enough. But not enough to blow up a decent Friday evening on meeting a few dozen people he didn't even know.

He was about to put the car in reverse and get out as soon as possible, when a group of girls caught his eye. They were emerging from a Brio a few cars ahead but it was the girl emerging from the driver's seat that held his attention.

He just couldn't believe his luck! It seemed as if the fate had determined to put her in front of him wherever he turned. Also, Piyush had also spotted him and was waving like a monkey to grab his attention. Oh well, you couldn't fight the Fates, could you?

Winters in Ranchi were usually a pleasant experience. There is a refreshing bite in the air and log drives even more fun. Unfortunately there is also a menace which most people also know as college. It was on such a day that Vidisha was looking out of the window of her classroom gazing at a leaf as it shed its tree and joined the carpet that lay at its base. She let out a long sigh and prayed for the class to end, wishing with every fibre of her being that she was outside.

Gradually Vidisha began to reminisce about Aarav's party. It had been great to catch up with old friends. The one surprise she received was to see Varun and Piyush there. Although it was kind of expected, seeing that there were around 200 people present. Varun was a different entity altogether. He made her feel different, weird, but not in a bad way. When he looked at her, all smoking hot and intense, Vidisha's tummy did a flop without fail. There was no doubt that Varun affected her. Its outcome, however, was yet to be seen. She had accepted Varun's friend request and suddenly, POOF, he was everywhere! Maybe the next time, they would be able to talk for more than a few minutes.

For a guy who hardly ever went to his own college, Varun sure as hell was spending a lot of time at Piyush's college. Today, he was here to pick up Piyush and no surprises; there was no sight of him. Frustrated, Varun reached out to kick the tire of his bike, missed and hit a brick instead. Cursing the pain, he was about to leave when he heard a sympathetic voice behind him, a voice (that had begun to haunt him in his dreams) that he found, he liked very much.

'Ouch! That must have hurt.'

He looked over and saw Vidisha and Piyush coming over to him. His grin was painful but it was a grin, nevertheless, Piyush, aka Certified Traitor, was laughing at his pain. His only balm was Vidisha's smile.

Vidisha left Varun and Piyush at the gate and wondered how she had gotten herself invited to a guy's birthday celebration whom she knew not more than 3 months ago. At first they joked with each other about Piyush's lamentable time management and then, out of nowhere Varun was asking Vidisha to come to his house this weekend. It was his birthday and a few of his friends would also join in. The only thing that was news to her and confirmed her answer was that Reva and a bunch of other college friends were also coming. She said yes, and went away, wondering, yet, very, very excited.

By the end of the weekend, Vidisha had made a friend; one whom she believed understood her very well. Varun turned out to be a very good host. His party was well-planned and he was attentive to all his guests. But that was not what had affected Vidisha.

An hour into the festivities, everyone was dancing. There were around 20–25 people and Vidisha had been acquainted with all of them. She had been dancing with Piyush, and Akriti, a friend of Varun's and now she wanted some fresh air, she had noticed small balcony near the upstairs lounge & beeline for it.

Easing out into the balcony Vidisha slipped out of her heels and took in the crisp evening air. She passed to admire her shoes for the evening which, were a lovely sea green coloured, strappy sandals. They went well with her pale pink skater dress. As Vidisha bent down to put them on the floor, she heard the door of the balcony open.

The scent hit her first. It had started to entice her and it belonged to just one guy, Varun.

She smiled as she turned around.

'Hey birthday boy' her voice became subconsciously husky.

'What are you doing out here? Is everything fine? Can I get you something?'

Vidisha smiled at his concern. She had started to find herself liking Varun's company, a lot. He entered the balcony and came to stand next to her. They talked about a lot of things.

The first time they met (they laughed a lot over that) the second time they met (they laughed even harder). Like on the night of the fest, the two lost track of time. They talked and they opened. They blossomed and they grew closer.

When Vidisha casually mentioned going back inside, Varun stayed put and drew her back into the conversation. Vidisha agreed.

Vidisha remembered the hours they spent talking, even after the party broke up, Varun somehow had her number and even after she went home, they talked and texted for hours.

Hours turned into days, days into weeks and weeks into months. Never a day went by when they didn't talk. Not a week passed where they didn't meet. They made time for each other and gradually they became as integral to each other's life.

They were friends, friends who were wildly, madly, passionately in love with each other. But neither could express this love for fear of losing their friendship. It wouldn't be long before they reach their breaking point. The question is who would do it first?

6

CARS AND ROSES!

The clock struck at midnight. Vidisha's mouth was full of cake and her face looked like one. Her brother had spread half the icing on her face and was now laughing like a baboon. Her mom and dad were hugging her and wishing her happy birthday.

On her night stand her cell phone was ringing and flashing a name: Varun.

Vidisha picked up a huge chunk of cake and started to run after her brother. Their parents were laughing, with her dad encouraging Viaan to go hide somewhere and mom admonishing them to act like adults.

Her cell phone was still ringing and it was Varun.

Vidisha and Viaan came out of the washroom after cleaning their faces. Their clothes were a mess. Her parents had already gone to bed. Viaan wished her once again and he too went to bed. Vidisha changed out of her chocolate smeared clothes and put on a fresh pair of

PJ's. With a huge smile on her face she laid down of her bed. The sudden vibrations of her cell startled her, she checked her phone; it was Saket calling.

"Hey granny, how many more years do you have to live?" he said without any preamble.

"Hey yourself asshole, I'll probably die the day after you do"

"Hahahahaha… A very happy birthday princess"

"Thanks yaar. You are the first to call me, Jerk face Reva must be snoring the night away I don't even think she knows it's my birthday today."

In her mind she was thinking why Varun hasn't called yet.

"You know how she is like; every year you're the one who ends up calling her and asking her to wish you."

"I know, I'll go buzz her. Thanks Saket, good night. Bye!"

After hanging up, Vidisha speed dialled Reva. Five and a half rings later a sleepy Reva picked up.

"You better have a fucking good reason to be waking me up at 1 in the night. Either state your business in the next five seconds or get the fuck lost." She slurred.

"The fucking good reason I have, is that it's my birthday, you bitch! I shouldn't have to be the one to call you!"

"Oh damn! That's today!? Ok. Please text me the venue and the time. See you in the evening. Bye!" saying so she hung up.

Vidisha looked at her cell in mock horror, with her mouth hanging open. Despite that she couldn't help the smile on her face. Damn she loved her friends.

Checking her cell, she saw that she had around seven missed calls from Varun. Holy Shit…!!!!

She quickly called him back and he immediately picked up. Before he could say anything she launched into a huge and elaborate apology.

"I'm so sorry. I just saw your calls now. I was all covered in chocolate and mom and dad were in the room and I had to kick Reva's ass for not wishing me…"

"Whoa, whoa, whoa. Hold your horses, sweetheart. There's no need to get hyper. It's all right. By the way, happy birthday to the most beautiful girl in my world."

Vidisha blushed. He said the sweetest things sometimes.

"Thank you" Vidisha stifled a huge yawn.

"Hmm…go to sleep. I'll talk to you tomorrow. Sweet dreams baby."

Next morning Vidisha got up to the heavenly aroma of hot coffee. She saw the maid Sukhmani, holding a large cup of coffee.

"Happy birthday didi."

Vidisha took the cup from her and welcomed the boost of caffeine. She thanked Sukhmani and propped herself on the pillows. On her night stand were three perfectly wrapped gifts. Opening them she found a sexy Fossil watch, a book,'Those Pricey Thakur Girls' by Anuja Chauhan (this was definitely her mom's gift) and an empty box that had a note: "*You really expected a gift?!'*– Love, your darling brother'.

As she entered college, a few of her class mates came to wish her. She also had a number of posts on her Facebook wall. As she entered the class she saw Reva sitting on her desk and haranguing Atul, one of the sweetest guys in her class.

"You asshole, Reva Narayan!" Vidisha shouted.

"Oh look who can legally drink now! Darling, we are so getting wasted today…" The rest of Reva's words were muffled as she drowned Vidisha in a hug of ginormous proportions.

"Ya right, like that's going to happen." But sure, we'll *pakka* party today."

The rest of the day passed in a routine of boring classes and even more boring professors. At 12:30 when her last class got over Vidisha was ready to call it quits.

She had planned to meet up with a bunch of her friends at The Vanilla Bean, a sexy coffee place at around 1.30.

She went home and changed into a pretty dress. The dress was a gift from one of her cousins. It was a delicate blush colour and fit her like a glove. It had a full skirt and danced around her knees like a permanent wind was blowing. She probably looked like a princess and definitely felt like one.

As she went out, she called her mom to inform her of her plans. The moment she hung up, Varun called her.

"Hey sweetness, wassup?" she asked him.

"What are you doing right now?" his tone had an urgency that worried her.

"I'm just leaving for lunch with the girls. What happened Varun?"

"Nothing to worry about, I was just wondering if you could meet me now."

"Now? As in now, now?"

"Yeah. Please, I want to be with you on your special day. Trust me; you won't regret it for a second."

Damn that guy was good. Vidisha melted all over again and agreed to meet him. He would be picking her in 10 minutes.

Vidisha knew she would be in hot water as she dialled Reva's number. She knew that she was being a bitch but in this case, cute guy definitely trumped childhood friend.

"Yeah babes, I'm almost ready. I'll be there in thirty." Reva said as she picked the call.

'Fucking hell!!' Vidisha thought. She was so screwed.

"Yeaaaaah. About that. Ummm. You know… I really wanted to go and it happened just so suddenly, you know how much I love you, right? And it's not that I don't want to go…"

"Whoa, whoa, whoa. Slow down Quickgun Murugan. Lemme guess? You have a date with Varun, don't you? Ditching your friends for a guy won't get you anywhere Miss Vidisha Agarwal."

Fuck. That was the problem of being so close to some people that you can't even lie to them.

"I'm so sorry Reva. I promise I'll make it up to you guys; you name it and it's yours. And it's not really a date. Come on, we are just going out as friends."

"Uh-huh. And denial is a river in Egypt. Anyways, because I happen to be an awesome person, plus it is your birthday, you get a jail-free pass. Now, get lost bitch. And make me proud!"

Vidisha gave Reva a huge sloppy phone kiss and said, "You are the most fucking awesome friend in the whole wide world, Reva. Had I not been straight I would totally have kissed you."

"I know, I know. You can make it up by giving me good, juicy details when you get back. Bye."

Vidisha hung up and dashed back inside. She gave herself an onceover in the mirror. The dress was perfect. The only change she made was that she swapped her stilettos for a pair of sexy ballerinas. Fifteen minutes later she heard the honk of a car. Locking the door behind her, she dashed down the driveway and into his car.

Varun was dressed casually in a pair of blue denims and a white comfort T. He had put on a pair of purple rimmed Ray-Bans Vidisha was immediately lusting after. Right now, those Ray-Bans as well as his mouth were hanging in loose air. Vidisha was vain enough to cheer mentally on seeing his reaction. Varun gave a low wolf-whistle and said'

"Darling, I think that today it might be might my birthday rather than yours." The entire time his eyes were on her.

The blush on Vidisha's cheeks turned three shades darker.

"Shut up and drive, you moron."

"Your wish is my command, my lady. Just tell me where you want to go."

"Hey it's your call. Wherever you want; it's fine by me."

"Come on, you're the birthday girl. Tell me where to go."

"Ummm… I seriously can't think of any place right now."

"Oh please! There must be some place you want to be."

This argument continued for another twenty minutes. The entire time Varun was driving around aimlessly. Finally when Vidisha was starting to lose her temper, Varun stopped the car by the side of the road. Vidisha looked around. They had crossed the Dhurwa industrial sector moments ago. But as she looked about, Vidisha saw that she was not at all familiar with the area.

"Ummm… Varun where are we?"

"I don't know. I just stopped the car. You were the one who could not decide where to go."

"Excuse me? Are you telling me that we are stranded in the middle of nowhere?"

Varun gave a naughty grin and Vidisha immediately understood that this was a prank. "You stupid jerk; I was scared shitless for a second. Don't do that ever again."

"I won't if you'll do one thing for me. Would you please wear this and sit still for 5 minutes." He pulled out a pretty silk scarf and waved it in front of her.

Instantly Vidisha was curious and apprehensive all at once.

" Varun, what exactly are you doing?"

"Please yaar, just trust me once. I promised this to you before that I am not a pervert or a rapist."

"Ya right! Like any rapist would admit that!"

Muttering under her breath, Vidisha turned so that he could tie the silk scarf he had taken out from his pocket.

He wrapped it around her eyes firmly but not too tightly. "Now sit still."

Vidisha was very intrigued as to what he was doing. She could hear him opening the boot, then there were a few rustling sounds. 2 minutes later she heard the hiss of a match stick and the pungent odour of lit sulphur reached her nose.

Another minute later she heard Varun come by her side and open the car door. With one arm gently holding her arm, he carefully eased her out.

"That's it, we are almost there!"

He stood her firmly and with a flourish he removed the scarf from Vidisha's eyes.

Vidisha could not help the gasp that came out of her mouth; such was the beauty of the scene in front of her. The back of Varun's car looked like a dream.

There were balloons framing the boot. On its floor was a pretty little cake topped with a multitude of candles. Next to the cake was a small pile of carefully wrapped gifts.

Vidisha could not help the tears that came to her eyes. This was the most thoughtful thing that anyone had ever done for her. Varun's hands were still on her shoulders and she could gauge that he was a little tensed awaiting her reactions. She turned and engulfed him in a warm hug.

She put forth everything she wanted to say and could not, into that hug.

Breaking apart they gave each other goofy smiles.

"Come on, the candles are melting." He led her to the car and they sat in the remaining space.

She blew out the candles and Varun sang for her. Vidisha had to admire his attention to detail. He even had a spoon for them to eat the cake. He fed the first bite to her. The cake was her favourite, chocolate ganache. The next few moments were spent in talking and feeding each other bits of cake.

"Hey! Don't you want to open your gifts?

"Shit! I completely forgot. Hell yeah! I'm super excited!!"

Vidisha barely stopped herself from attacking the wrapping paper. The first was a cute little stuffed cat which had patches all over it. Next was a top in vibrant jewel tones which Varun said reminded him of her. She also got two large Silks and the best was a book, Bed Of Roses by Nora Roberts.

Vidisha couldn't help herself. She jumped up and hugged Varun once again. On an impulse she kissed him on the cheek. Uh - oh. They moved away, but the atmosphere was little awkward. Varun cleared his throat and tried to lighten the atmosphere.

"Hey, you didn't see your final gift. Vidisha looked up to see him holding a blood-red rose liberally sprinkled with silver glitter.

"'Thank you Varun". Taking the rose from him, Vidisha continued. "And not just for all this. You are so, so special to me. You have no idea how drastically you've changed me and my life."

"Come on, don't get sentimental. I am just doing what a good friend does. Now come on its time for lunch." Right on cue a delivery guy from Dominos came up to them.

"Special order for Miss Vidisha Agarwal" he pulled out a pizza box with great flourish.

Vidisha could only look at him with eyes as big as saucers. She watched dumbstruck as Varun paid the guy and took the pizza from him. Varun turned to her with a look of great pride and satisfaction.

"How on earth did you manage all this?" the dumbfounded tone did not go waste on Varun. There was a pleasure that was so obvious on her lovely face that it made everything worthwhile.

"I hope you like jalapeno and red pepper. Now say aaaaah…"

Without thinking Vidisha opened her mouth and Varun popped an entire slice of smoking hot pizza in it.

"Oh shit! It's so damn hot." Vidisha glared daggers at him as she mentally heaved a sigh of relief that the hot pie had freed her from that cyclone of emotions that threatened to engulf her. Varun had also somehow managed to conjure two Cokes out from his magic bag of tricks. They enjoyed the food in companionable silence. They finished the last slice watching the sunset and the sky engulfed in fire.

The drive home was passed in both of them lost in their own thoughts. Vidisha had noticed that throughout their day Varun kept touching his jeans' pocket. She dismissed it without another thought. She was still hugging the cat that was sitting in her lap. The rest of her gifts were in a carry bag in the back seat. As they made the turn for her house, Vidisha noticed Varun getting more and more fidgety. He kept on looking at her like a gaping fish counting its last breaths. Vidisha became a little concerned but they had almost reached her home. She turned to him and was almost about to ask him what the matter was when he spoke.

"Vidisha…" his voice came out on a strangled choke. He tried again. "Vidisha, there's something…" his voice trailed off.

She waited for a few moments but when he did not seem to go on she prodded him, "Yes Varun, I'm waiting. Tell me."

"I, I umm…you see, there's actually…" Vidisha had never seen him this nervous.

"Oh to hell with it!!" the note of frustration was evident in his voice. She looked to see him draw another gift-wrapped box from his jeans.

"Oh my God, Varun! Are you crazy? You've already given me so much. This is really not necessary. Please."

But she was already unwrapping the gift. Inside it was a flat jeweller's box made out of fine blue velvet. Vidisha's breath hitched. Oh dear God, it better not be what she thought it was. She watched in mild horror as he threw away the paper and opened the box. The pressure in her lungs eased when she saw that it was a pretty charm bracelet. The bracelet had a beaten silvery tint; from it hung a number of charms. On closer inspection she saw a tiny kitten frolicking, a bottle which she had to assume was vodka. There was also a miniature car, a teeny tiny rose and finally a V, which obviously meant Vidisha, right? It was breath-taking.

"Varun!" Vidisha's breath escaped on a sigh. No matter how beautiful, she really, really could not accept this thoughtful gift. They all were things that she had done with Varun. Him, calling her a wildcat, the vodka they stole, the car ride home and the rose, Gulabi Ankhen. "I really can't."

"Please Vidisha, if not for you, then for me at least." Before she could say anything, he took her hand and was fastening the bracelet on her wrist. This time Vidisha did not try to stop the tears that came to her.

"Oh, Vidisha? One more thing." She looked at him expectantly.

"I love you."

7

THE YOUNG AND THE RECKLESS

Vidisha woke up the next morning feeling all sorts of guilty. Dammit, why the hell was she the one who was feeling this way? She was not the one who had to propose out the blue. Her face flushed in remembering last night's memories. Her looking at Varun with undiluted shock. He looking back at her with an annoyingly patient look. As if he was completely sure of her acquiescence. Damn the guy was too cocky for his own good. Who the fuck asked him to go and screw her life like this? She had been perfectly happy before he dropped his cute little, charm bracelet-covered bomb over her. So what, if for the first time in her life, she was feeling complete? So what, if Varun made her feel special, and beautiful, and cherished? So what, if she too wanted him so bad, it hurt?

Vidisha fell back on the pillows like a deflated balloon. Yup, she was screwed and she knew it. She suddenly got up again. 'No! No! I have plans. I have major career and life plans and no guy is messing them up. I will not let him.'

She lay down on the bed again and massaged her eyes. Flashbacks of yesterday ran through her mind.

Had Vidisha known that she was looking like a goldfish with her mouth an O of surprise, she might have been amused. But her brains were totally scrambled. For several moments she just stared at Varun, unable to utter a single word. He was holding her hand and was idly playing with the charms on her bracelet. The bracelet! The one he gave to her. Vidisha jolted out of her reverie and started to gather her stuff- the cat, the book, the bag containing the shirt, the rose, not realising that she was almost frantic in her attempt to get out. The third time she tried, and failed, to open the door, Varun leaned over and opened it. Vidisha scrambled out.

"Umm thanks, bye. Yeah, I've gotta go. See you. Okay, I'm going. Bye, I've already said that. OK." And without looking back, Vidisha dashed into the safety of her home...

But before she reached the door, Varun called out to her. Helpless, she turned around.

"I'll be waiting for your answer."

Vidisha seriously considered going back to sleep again. Facing the world was so not on her to-do list. Shit! Could that have been any more embarrassing? College was over, she had her exams way ahead in June and before that, two whole months of bliss. But, as she was snuggling deeper in the covers, an avalanche in the form of one, annoying Reva Narayan, crashed down on her. The only thing saving Vidisha from several broken bones was the number of pillows which cushioned Reva's launch by several degrees. Still, she could not stop the groan that escaped from her mouth.

"I hate you, you bitch. Why the hell are you here, messing up my morning?"

"Well, good morning to you too, sunshine. You see, I am after all your best friend. It is my sacred duty and birth right to make sure you pay for ditching your friends and depriving us out of cake, you moron."

"Cut it out, Reva. Your voice is hurting my ears."

"Aww, too bad. Now, if you are not up and ready in thirty, you'll be missing your own birthday party."

That certainly, was more effective than a bucket of ice water. Vidisha sat up at once.

"Party? *My* party? As in a party just for me? Are you fucking serious? Oh my god! Tell me you're serious?"

"Yeah, yeah." Reva's tone was the perfect combination of pride and excitement. "When I Whatsapped everyone to cancel yesterday, they were pretty pissed off. So, to appease them I began to blab about a house party in the works. Well, one thing led to another and we somehow ended up planning to get together at Ritika's place. Her parents are out of town for the week. She has the house all to herself, or, should I say, us."

Vidisha was one of those persons who usually never ran out of words, but at that moment, she could not, for the love of God, string a coherent statement. Next, she and Reva were jumping on her bed, screaming at the top of their lungs. Vidisha's mom peeked into the room the din they made could be heard from miles. Smiling slightly, she left the two friends basking in the joys of being young.

A few minutes later, they both fell, breathless, on the bed. When they could breathe properly, Reva kicked Vidisha.

"Move your ass, fatso. We have to be at Ritika's by 11:30. We also have to pick up the cigarettes and the wafers on the way."

Yawning and struggling to disentangle herself from the sheets, Vidisha hauled herself to the bathroom. She came out, her mouth full of toothpaste and was not at all surprised to see Reva putting on a top from her wardrobe. "Take something out for me too." and Vidisha went to take a quick shower.

Ritika's house was almost on the outskirts of Ranchi. Since the drive would be long, they opted to take Vidhi's car. They took a slight detour to pick up the smokes and the chips were on the way to her house. On the way, Vidisha filled in the incidents of yesterday to Reva. And Reva for a change was the perfect audience. She was equally shocked and supportive. But her one comment had Vidisha thinking. As Vidisha was telling her how adorably frustrated Varun was, Reva said,

"But darling, are you really surprised? I mean, come on, you and Varun were literally attached at the hip from the moment you guys met. And would it really be a wrong thing to be in a relationship. You have never been in a serious one and Varun is really nice. We all like him. Plus you guys look really cute together."

Feeling a bit relieved that she had, at least, *one* of her closest friend's blessing, Vidisha made the turn into Ritika's drive.

They were not very late, but when they entered the house, they found a veritable feast had been spread. Of course, it was not your typical food fiesta. The dining table would not have looked out of place in a bar. Vodka to whisky, you name it and you had it. Reva explained that half of them had pinched their dads' stash and the rest had chipped in to buy the remaining booze.

Priyanka and Soumya were in charge of the drinks. They were looking up recipes for a cornucopia of cocktails. Ritika and Purva were setting up the music system. The sultry tones of 'Babydoll' could be heard over the din that was being made. In the kitchen, Sarah was putting candles on an enormous chocolate cake. None of them had noticed Vidisha and Reva entering. After standing for two minutes without being noticed, Reva finally had enough. Her "Hello, bitches" was loud enough for everyone to notice them. After the initial blank faces, they all caught up and screamed in perfect sync.

"SURPRISE!"

Despite the delayed reaction, Vidisha could not help the joy that flooded through her. Damn, her friends were awesome!

Laughing, they closed the door and went to make a few drinks for themselves.

An hour later, Vidhi had a vodka martini in her hand and a plastic tiara on her head, courtesy of Priyanka. The rest of them were wearing party hats and were totally, completely drunk. An empty bottle of Coke was rolling in the floor. Reva was in the kitchen heating the coal for the hookah. Vidisha was sitting on the floor and Sarah had her head in her lap. They were both sharing a cigarette. Some idiot had gone and put on cheesy, sappy romantic songs on the stereo. After the second time, 'Bhul Ja' came on, Vidisha had had enough.

"For God's sake! Can someone please switch off this shit? I can take no more of heartbreak and emotional trauma."

Laughing, Purva went and changed the track. The upbeat strains of Charlie XCX's 'I Don't Care' were a welcome change and the mood began to lift. First, Reva and Ritika got up and started to dance together. Although 'dance' was a very loose term for what they were really doing. It looked more like a strip show, minus the removal of clothes. Soumya had somehow managed to find some Monopoly money and when the track changed to '*Beedi Jalayle*' she started to rain the cash on them.

The rest of them almost died laughing. Vidisha had a stitch in her side from laughing so long and so hard. Somebody whistled, but by now, they were too sloshed to pay attention. Priyanka got up and pulled Vidhi and Sarah to their feet. For a few moments they were lost in dance and music, celebrating so many things; Vidisha's birthday, a chance to feel free and give reign to all their desires which Indian society takes special pleasure in squashing. Despite Ranchi's beauty, it was still not a place where a girl could smoke or drink in public. It was also a celebration of the end of their college days. Most of them would be going away for further studies, or at the least changing colleges. Sarah was going to Chennai to pursue a journalism course, Vidisha planned to apply for courses in several designing colleges. Reva had decided to opt for Masters in Computer applications. Priyanka and Purva were both studying for MBA. It felt like an era had passed. It was a step into the real world for them. It was both exhilarating and bittersweet.

Suddenly, from behind them, Ritika got out the cake and was lighting what seemed like hundreds of candles.

"Happy Birthday, Darling!"

Vidisha laughed and was dragged to the table. The cake looked as if it could have fed at least an entire herd of elephants. Vidisha looked at her friends through the warm glow of the candles. Reva was mouthing at her to make a wish, but at that moment she felt utterly content. A second later, she involuntarily desired that this would have been perfect had she had Varun by her side. Varun. He was as integral a part of her life as any. Closing her eyes, Vidisha made her wish…

By 6:30, it was time to wrap up the party. Because Soumya and Sarah stayed in hostels, they were spending the night at Ritika's. Priyanka's boyfriend was coming to pick her up and he would also be dropping off Purva. Vidisha and Reva had stopped drinking a few hours ago because one, Vidisha was driving and two; Reva parents would kill her if she came home high as a kite.

They helped Ritika clean up the mess they had made. Empty bottles were stacked in a corner, to be disposed of in the morning. Ashtrays were flushed down, glasses washed multiple times to remove the smell of alcohol, empty cigarette cartons and pizza boxes were thrown in the trash and the living room sprayed with an entire can of deodorant. In the end Soumya had had too much to drink and she was passed out in Ritika's bed. Priyanka was lying on the floor and had a half empty bottle of beer in her hand. Her parents were both working and came home late. So she had no issue on reaching home drunk.

With a final goodbye, Vidisha Reva went to the car. After dropping of Reva, Vidisha came home to find that her mom was out with her brother. Sukhmani was preparing dinner and was murdering a Shreya Ghoshal song. Heaving a sigh of relief that she would not have to face an irate parent, Vidisha trudged up to her room.

She brushed her teeth and changed into her PJs. She switched on her laptop and tried to concentrate on some last minute details for a wedding sangeet she was an event coordinator for. But no matter how hard she tried she could not get Varun out her mind. His parting words still echoed in her mind. She picked up her cell; there were no texts or calls from him. This was a first because never had a day gone by when they hadn't communicated for an extended period of time. Vidisha realised that she was actually missing the conversations, the jokes, the arguments that she had with him. For a moment she considered calling him and sorting out the situation. She had her thumb in the call button but at the last moment she hesitated. Throwing her phone on the bed in frustration, Vidisha went downstairs to divert herself in mindless television.

By 10:30, Vidisha was going out her mind. Throughout dinner she was restless. Even her clueless brother had picked up on it and had asked her, in his own imaginative way, what the hell was pissing the shit out of her. Vidisha had cuffed him on his head and told him to mind his own goddamn business. She somehow ambled her way to bed and considered reading a new novel she had started. Ten minutes into the story, she threw down the book in frustration. Damn that stupid guy who made her fall in love with him. Startled, Vidisha scrambled out of her bed. Love? Oh no, no, no. She frantically searched for her cell. She had to call Varun right now. Fishing her phone out of her bag, she dialled Varun's number.

"Hello?"

"Hi Varun, it's me, Vidisha." Why was her voice so breathless?

"I know darling. I saw the caller ID."

"Umm, what are you doing." Vidisha knew she was faltering.

"What I am really doing is waiting for your answer."

"Yeah…about that…"

Vidisha's heart was now thundering in her ears. She opened her mouth…

Her answer came out in a whisper.

"Yes."

8

A STREETCAR NAMED DESIRE!

Vidisha picked up her phone. It was Varun.

The smile that came to her face was automatic. Who would have thought that being in a relationship would be so joyous?

"Hey what's up?" She said.

"Hey listen I was wondering what you were doing right now?" His voice was soft and slightly hesitant. It made Vidisha wonder what he was up to.

"Nothing I'm free, tell me what happened?"

"Go out for a drive with me now?" He asked.

Vidisha felt a tiny fluttering in her tummy as she quickly replied,

"Why not? I don't mind! But it will take me an hour or so. Ok?"

"Yeah sure, no problem, will 4 o'clock work for you?" Varun said.

"Yes, but are you going to tell me what's going on… you're acting a little weird."

"It's nothing. Chill darling. See you in an hour." Saying that, he hung up.

For a second, Vidisha stood staring at her cell blankly. She was really enjoying Varun's company more and more. She was still getting used to the idea of being in a relation with him.

Walking up to her closet, Vidisha mulled over what to wear. Although she was as comfortable with Varun as she was with Reva and Saket, she still liked to primp herself a little for him. It was her only concession to her feminine side, which she otherwise, squashed down quite successfully.

She picked out a loose floral tunic dress in a pretty shade of cream. It had tiny roses in varying shades of red and pink. This she teamed up with knee length leggings. A smudge of kajal, a brush of her gloss and she was ready to go.

She picked up her keys, wallet and bag, told her mom that she'd be back in an hour or two, and walked the short distance to the edge of her colony where she had told Varun to pick her up.

Because she was a little early, she had some time to think over her relation with Varun. She felt a really strong connection with him and was beginning to trust him in ways she had never trusted anyone before. He could make her melt with a single look and they already had several on-going private jokes which drove their friends crazy.

She had also noticed that he was very possessive of her. He did not like it when guys came up to her and flirted with her. He would make fun of her along with Reva but there was a strained forcefulness to his jokes. Whenever they went out, to either see a movie or generally hang out together, he never let her pay. It took a lot of threats and some physical violence to let her pay her share of the bill after which she had to spend a good day or two cajoling him to make him aware that she was an independent female. One of his sweetest habits which endeared him to her was that he always somehow managed to be next to her, regardless of the number of people they were with. Seeing him sitting next to her had become as obvious as breathing.

Vidisha smiled to herself. She was falling hard for him and she had no wish to stop.

The blaring sound of a horn broke her out of her reverie. She looked up to see Varun smiling at her and once again her tummy felt as if it was doing gymnastics.

"Hey dreamy head! Which world were you lost in? I've been calling out to you for the past five minutes and you were just standing there smiling at some random point in the distance. Tell me you were fantasizing about me. After all, I am the guy of your dreams."

Vidisha blushed hard. It seemed as if he had a direct hotline to her most private thoughts. Before he came closer to hitting the target she dispelled the atmosphere into something more light.

"Oh yeah baby. That's exactly what I was doing. Beating up the shit out of you is the dream." She fought hard not to laugh when she saw his ears turn an adorable shade of red. She failed and laughed her heart out at his embarrassment.

"Yeah yeah. Whatever. I wouldn't get too cocky if I were you. After all, you are at my mercy for the next few hours." Varun swiftly shifted into reverse and drove off towards the highway.

Half an hour into the drive, they were still talking a mile a minute. Even when they agreed to disagree, they would end their discussion on amicable terms. Vidisha loved that she could talk to him about anything and everything, be it the latest government scam or how they preferred their Maggi (she liked it with veggies and he liked it with cheese-the slob!)

Varun had taken them to the outskirts of the town. A new highway had been recently constructed which connected all the major exits of Ranchi. It was generally very quiet and isolated, but if you stuck to your vehicle it was all right. The lush landscape of the rustic countryside never failed to soar Vidisha's heart.

Rolling green fields dotted with grazing cattle, robust truckers sipping hot tea at roadside stalls, young girls dressed in colourful outfits, all were like a balm to Vidisha's city ravaged soul. As much as she loved the city and the myriad facilities it provided, these rare excursions to the lap of nature provided a welcome distraction. Being with Varun was an added bonus.

Right now, he was telling her some funny incident that had happened in his college today, involving three of his friends, some screwdrivers, the keys to the Professors' Lounge and four dislocated hips.

"...and by the time the ruckus died down and the carpenter had come, Mrs. Kumar was still helping Prof. Desai and Prof. Bose off the floor." His voice was full of mirth as he ended his tale.

Vidisha laughed along with him. It had been a long time since she had felt such a connection with any guy. Although she was a little wary, she dared to hope for something more.

Varun pulled the car to the side of the road. They got out and Vidisha saw that they were standing at the edge of a lake. This pool of water was surrounded by large piles of rocks of a stormy grey. At one side, a small pathway led to a small cliff. At the edge of the cliff, a lone tree stood sentinel over the silvery blue waters of the lake. The water was completely still and she could see the reflection of the setting sun like a glorious disc of burnt gold.

Vidisha gave a gasp at the beauty of the scene in front of her. She had crossed this area several times before but had never noticed this lake. It seemed as if Fate had meant for her to come to this enchanted place with Varun only. Turning to him, she saw him holding a large bag of wafers and two bottles of booze-a beer for him and a Breezer for her. She was touched to see that he had remembered her favourite flavour, Jamaican. She hated the taste of cranberry, it reminded her too much of cough syrup.

With a grin, he gently held her hand and they walked towards the tree. They sat down under its shade. Varun twisted the cap of her drink and handed it to her. Taking a long swig from his beer, he gave her a look that was part tenderness, and part something she did not wish to acknowledge. She quickly averted her eyes and tried to calm herself. The intensity died down and she could hear him clearing his throat. She could picture him shaking his head and running his fingers through his already wind-swept hair.

"Vidisha…" His voice was rough and unsteady as if he was forcing himself to speak.

She looked up and saw that he was a lot closer to her. She could see the tips of his lashes glistening in the fading sunlight. His eyes, a warm dark brown, the colour of dark chocolate, were looking at her as if she was the only girl in the world. His hand came up to entwine a lock of her hair around his finger. Using her hair he pulled her even closer to him. Their lips were almost touching and Vidisha closed her eyes. Just as they were about to kiss, the opening notes of ACDC's 'Highway to Hell' burst their little cocoon. Both of them jumped in the air and were as red as beets. Varun cursed loudly and pulled out his cell.

"Shit! It's Piyush. I'm sorry sweetheart, but I'll have to take this." He stood up and moved a little farther away.

Vidisha took in a long breath and tried to clear her senses. She leaned against the trunk of the tree and thought about what had almost happened. Her heart was pounding and she felt as if she had just run a marathon. She was suddenly aware of her surroundings. As much as she wanted to kiss Varun, in the middle of nowhere was not what she had in mind. She smiled to herself at the impulsive mistake she was just about to make.

She could hear him talking to Piyush about some important meeting he had to go to. It was obvious that Varun was controlling himself not to shout and hang up on him. For a second, Vidisha wondered if they would pick up where they had left, but she decided not to.

She saw Varun hang up the phone and come back to her. It looked like he too was equally flustered by what had transpired between them. He sat down beside her again and gave her his trademark lopsided grin. She noticed he didn't try to kiss her again and she was relieved. It was too soon and she wasn't ready. Instead they went back to their talk on each other's favourite bands.

Time flew by and they were lost in each other. It wasn't until Vidisha saw that the sun had almost set that she became aware of the time. She gave a sudden yelp and jumped up. She searched for her cell but couldn't find it. She realised she must have forgotten it in the car.

"Shit Varun!! It's really late! Oh God, I was supposed to be home by 6:00. I don't even know what time it is." She knew she was panicking but she was worried her mom might have gone ballistic by now.

Both of them practically ran to the car and as soon as she got in, she immediately checked her cell. Holy Crap! It was already 6:30 and she had 7 missed calls from her mom. Shushing Varun with one hand she hurriedly dialled her mom's cell. Within two rings, her mother picked and literally shouted into the speaker.

"Vidisha? Oh my God! Where on earth have you been? I was so worried. You are never late and you usually call if you are. You weren't even picking up your cell. When are you coming home?" Although her mom was the coolest, she expected Vidisha to be responsible and just let her know of her plans. And Vidisha being the mama's girl that she was followed that rule to a T.

Suddenly, her mom's voice started to break. She was losing network and the last words she could make out her mom yelling was, "You better have a damn good excuse when you're home, young lady!"

Her heart sank. She was in a huge, huge mess and the first thing to do was to get home.

"Drive, drive, drive!" She shouted to Varun, who most annoyingly, had a huge grin on his face. The jerk was fucking amused at her situation!

"Don't smile, drive!" She felt like banging her head on the dashboard.

"Oh God! I'm so screwed. You," She glared daggers at him, "it's all your fault. You were the one who wanted to meet me so urgently and now you will have to drop me home within 10 minutes. And STOP laughing!!" Vidisha was this close to succumbing to actual physical violence.

"All right, all right. Just relax darling. Here, listen to some music. Now close your eyes, take a deep breath and let me do the driving." Varun said.

"Are you FUCKING out of your mind?? The hell I am going to listen to anything, to you or your crap music. And please, please drive faster."

"Sweetheart, you don't need to shout. I can hear you just fine. And there's nothing to be worried about. If you can't call your mom then text her. Tell her that you had to go to college for some last minute work and that your cell was silent and in your bag. Apologise, I'm sure she'll understand."

"Yeah, right. That's easy for you to say. You're not the one who is going to get a lecture on responsibility and how to be a good daughter." She retorted.

Varun chuckled, "Either ways sweetheart. What do you have to lose?"

"No Varun. I swear, if you do not get me home in ten minutes max, you are going to regret it so bad. I am this close to resorting to actual physical violence and right now I wouldn't even feel guilty. Oh God, oh God, oh God!!"

"Ok, you know what? That's it! Either you stop getting hyper now, or I'll make you." Varun looked like he had a devilish plan in his mind as he said this. But Vidisha was too worried to register his gaze properly.

"Make me? Oh, I'd like to see you try. How about you drive a little faster and keep your mouth shut!" This time even she was aware that her voice had shot up by several octaves.

Suddenly, Varun pulled hard to the side of the road. He screeched the tyres and stopped the car with a jerk. Turning to her, he gritted out, "I told you I'd shut you up." And loosening her seat belt, he pulled her to him and kissed her squarely on her mouth.

Vidisha was stunned speechless. Tingles of electricity shot throughout her being. She just could not believe that he was kissing her. One of his hands was clinched tightly around her waist. The other was spread over her neck and was pushing her mouth to his. The spicy scent of his cologne enveloped all around her. She was unable to move and she gave herself up to the magic that was happening in the confined spaces of the car.

Once her initial shock passed, she started to respond to the movements of his lips. She put her hand on his heart and was pleased to notice that it was beating as wildly and erratically as hers. The other she entangled in his soft, unruly hair and used it to grip him harder.

His tongue swept the seam of her lips and she opened them to grant him entry. His tongue teased hers and she shivered violently. Vidisha could feel tiny shocks wherever he touched her. He was caressing her so gently and she had never felt like this before. Was this what love felt like?

After what seemed to be an eternity, but was probably moments, they both pulled apart. They were breathing heavily and their clothes and hair were quite dishevelled. Varun's eyes were closed but his smile showed his utter pleasure in the moment. Opening them, he looked at her with a look that stole her breath. Gently, he refastened her seatbelt and turned on the ignition. Neither of them said a word, they didn't need to. Vidisha ran her tongue over her lips. She could taste his essence on them. Casting a furtive glance at him, she saw that he too was smiling like crazy. Blushing really hard, she turned her head and tried to concentrate on the boring stretch of road ahead of her.

His rich chuckle was like music to her ears. "Ignoring me won't make me go away, baby."

Vidisha blushed even harder and he laughed out loud.

"Gods you're gorgeous when you blush. You are red all over, even your hands, and love, even your eyes are blushing. You seriously blush all over." He lifted his hand from the gearshift and brushed his fingers over her cheek.

By this time, they had reached her house and Varun parked the car discreetly in a dark spot. He turned to her and looking straight into her eyes, said "I know I don't tell you this as much as I should, but Vidisha Agarwal, you are the best thing that has ever happened to me. I love you so much that, at times, it hurts."

Vidisha felt tears well up in her eyes. This was not one of the casual 'I love yous said just for the heck of it. The emotion behind his words moved her to the core.

"I love you too, Varun, so much. And I am so happy you came to me that day and asked me for directions. Because, had that not happened, I never would have known what true happiness could feel like."

She hugged him tightly and got out of the car. As she entered home, she wasn't even aware of her mother scolding her. She listened half-heartedly to her mom, because her entire being craved to be with the man who had stolen her heart.

9

INFINITE CHAOS

After two years of loving someone with everything she had, Vidisha never even dreamt of a life where Varun would not be with her. By the end of that morning Vidisha had never hated anything as much as she was beginning to hate an orthodox society and match making aunts.

She had actually been looking forward to the day. It was a rare holiday for her and she was taking the opportunity to sleep in. So, by the time she woke up and got dressed it was almost 11 o'clock. As she came out of her room, she was delighted to see her aunt, Asha sitting at the dining table and enjoying a cup of tea with her mom.

"Hey, *Bua*, how come you are here so early?

"Early? Beta, you'll also have to learn to get up early once you are married."

Vidisha cringed mentally. She loved most of her extended family but Asha *bua* had a knack of pushing all the wrong buttons. She was one of those old school matronly types who believed that getting married into a "good house" was the greatest achievement for any girl. She had got her own daughter married at the age of 22. Now, her cousin who used to excel at literature had to give up her dreams of being a professor and work on being an "ideal bahu", somehow is the one who stays at home, all day long, working in the kitchen.

But because she was pondering over the injustice that most Indian women had to face, Vidisha missed what the adults were talking about. It was only when she looked up to see her mother and aunt wearing identical maniacal grins that she sensed something wrong.

"Umm, okay? What are you two plotting? And stop looking at me like that, it's seriously creepy." Vidisha looked in between the two of them. Her aunt wore an expression of such immense pride and her mom was smiling like crazy. Suddenly much to Vidisha's horror tears began to null in her mother's eyes. "Oh my god! Ma, what happened? Why are you crying?"

Vidisha felt herself go numb at her mother's next words.

"Well, it's not every day that your only daughter gets married, is it?"

There was a strong hollow feeling in her gut and for a moment she felt like throwing up. Such was her shock that she had trouble taking in air. She forced herself to break out of her daze and talk to them.

"You're kidding, right? I'm only twenty two. It almost is equivalent to child marriage. And seriously mom when did you start getting so excited over the getting me married off so soon?"

"Oh sweetie! It's not that i am asking you to get married today itself. Asha just came to tell me and your papa about this amazing *rishta* she has got for you."

"Yes beta, these people I am talking about are very nice. I have met the boy's parents and I must tell you that they are such *khandani* people. If you go there you will live like a princess.

Vidisha stared blindly at her aunt, the blood rushing in her ears. Marriage? To someone who was not Varun? Goosebumps broke over her skin and she was wracked by a sudden bout of shivers. Somehow, just barely, she managed to regain control over herself.

"*Bua* i don't really care how his parents are, i have dreams to fulfil and marriage at the age of twenty two is just not one of them. I haven't even finished my design course yet, and even after that i want to work on it even more. How can you even think about such stuff right now?"

Her aunt's reply was stern and quite serious.

"Vidisha, you are just a child. As adults we know what's best for you. One, you are twenty two. What, will you wait until you are old? And beta, *tum ladki ho*. You have to leave and go to your new home. Make a family and have a kid, that is your ultimate responsibility."

In her mind, Vidisha was screaming herself hoarse. She had never been overly fond of her aunt and right now, she outright hated her. She clenched her jaw to stop her teeth from chattering and placed her hands under the table where her mother wouldn't see them shaking. Her eyes were burning with unshed tears and she drew in a ragged breath to calm herself. She turned to her mom.

"Are you seriously telling me that you guys are actually considering this utter nonsense?" she ignored her aunts offended gasp.

"Vidisha! Don't talk like that! And stop being so dramatic. It's not like we're forcing you. We are just considering options here. There is no need to react like a spoilt child."

Astonished, Vidisha retorted, "Wow, mom! At least make up your mind. Either I'm a child who can't even think for itself or I'm an adult who can shoulder all the responsibilities of marriage. What am I, mom?"

She almost shouted the last part and jumping out of her chair she ran to the refuge of her room. She subconsciously wiped away the tears that she didn't even know was falling. She heard the faint voice of her aunt assuring her mother to let her be.

Once inside the room Vidisha's first reaction was to call Varun. Fishing out her cell, she hesitated over Varun's speed dial. But she could not bring herself to call him no matter how desperately she wanted to talk to him. She looked at the clock. He would be in office right now and wouldn't be able to pick up her call. That was a good thing, Vidisha mused. It would give her time to calm herself. She could not bring herself to drop this bomb on him when she herself was so fragile at this moment.

Knowing her aunt, she was sure that her mother had to listen to a lot of bitter things. Tentatively, she sat down at the table. Hesitantly, she called out to her mother.

'Mumaa!'

As her mother looked at her, Vidisha was slightly relieved to see her mom looking at her with love and acceptance. That itself went a long way to ease Vidisha's heart.

By noon she had a slight headache and just wanted to take a nap. Two hours later she was feeling a little better. She washed her face and came out of her room. Her aunt had left and it looked like her mom had been crying. A pang of guilt speared through Vidisha. Her mom smiled tentatively at her and Vidisha eased up a little. The awkwardness was still there and Vidisha was relieved when lunch was over.

Once in her room Vidisha texted Varun,

'Hey, how are you?'

'I miss you!'

'I love you'.

Fifteen minutes later, Varun replied,

Are you Okay? Is everything Alright?'

She answered 'Yes'

Back in Mumbai Varun felt a sense of unease creep up. But he couldn't dwell on it the moment because his supervisors was calling him.

As evening approached, both lovers had a sense of foreboding. Varun called Vidisha and for ten minutes they were just skirting around the issue. Finally, Varun had enough.

"What is it Vidisha, will you tell me?"

And Vidisha blurted out, "Asha *Bua* got a marriage proposal for me today."

For a moment, silence reigned.

"Varun? Varun ! Say something."

"When did this happen?" His tone had completely changed.

As Vidisha narrated the entire tale, she could sense Varun pulling farther away from her. In the end she couldn't even hear him breathing. After what felt like eons, he said, in a hoarse voice,

"I think we should break-up."

For the second time in the day Vidisha felt like throwing up. Her phone clattered to the floor and her knees gave out. She hadn't cried the entire day and now she curled up on the floor, gut wrenching sobs wracking her body. Vidisha let herself sink into oblivion.

10

A MAN'S NEED FOR LOGIC

Men have very simple needs. They can make do with a limited amount of clothes. They don't need to post every little aspect of their lives on social media. Except for the occasional porn, they are pretty much in control of their hormones. Why waste words when your work can be done with a few grunts and backslaps. Yeah, men had an inclination towards peace and logic. That was what Varun believed.

Now women, they were an entirely different matter. 'Simple' never exists in their dictionary. Why do something easily when you can add a truckload of melodrama in it? And selfie's, don't even get started on them. From the moment they are conscious, till the wee hours of the night, they have photographic evidence to document every single moment of their day. Again, this was what Varun believed. But this was before he met Vidisha. Not that Vidisha had not done any of the above mentioned things. Varun loved her with the entire fibre of his being but even he dreaded Vidisha's monthly mood swings.

They both had their faults but when they were together, the both of them they were flawless. Being with Vidisha made Varun want to be a better man. Two years down into their relationship and Varun still fell for her like he had one magical night long ago.

That day, he had woken up from a particularly steamy dream involving Vidisha and a jumbo size jar of chocolate sauce. Taking the dream as a good omen, he woke, stile smiling at the remnants of the fading dream. There was never a time when he had hated the damn distance between Mumbai and Ranchi.

He was humming '*Gulabi Ankhen*' the entire time he was getting dressed and was, in general, so annoyingly happy that even his roommates joined in his cheerful mood. Yes, life sure was going good. Too bad it was going to shatter all around him.

His good mood carried on with him till the better part of the day. It wasn't until around two that the first stirrings of unease started to creep around. Generally, Vidisha would have sent him some stupid, cheesy yet entirely lovable text by now. Not that it meant anything was wrong, but those had become such an integral part of his routine that he missed their arrival. Just as he was thinking about calling on buzzing her, a text pinged on his cell phone.

'Hey, how are you?'

It was Vidisha. Varun smiled, think about an angel....

Then his phone buzzed again, and then again.

'I Miss you!'

'I Love you.'

Varun frowned. This was not her usual MO. He couldn't exactly pinpoint it but he could almost sense a melancholic note of despair in the text. The back of his neck which had been tingling settled but a huge weight in his chest weighed him down. Looking down at his cell, he was shocked to see his hand trembling. Hastily, he typed a response asking whether everything was alright. Two minutes later, her clipped, short, 'Yes' sent him into further worry. Just as he was about to call her, one of his seniors called him over for some work. He out his cell away and went to work, his mind and heart equally heavy.

By the end of the day, Varun's nerves were frazzled. Threads of agitation ran throughout his body. He had been thinking of all sorts of scenarios, ranging from bad phase, he had nightmarish visions of a world where he couldn't be with Vidisha. He was just 23 years old. Marriage? That was something he didn't even consider. Right now, he had himself. And, he didn't even want to think about this part, what if her parents reject him just because he was not of their caste?

Will they accept a guy who is yet to gain his name and fame in the society and moreover is a non- Marwari? Varun's imaginations were delving into completely darker territories. Finally, after hyperventilating for about an hour, he forced himself to calm down and logically, like a man.

For the first time in two years Varun actually thought about where their relationship was heading. There was no doubt that he loved Vidisha, but what about their future? He knew that some people settled down early in life but he was not among them. Maybe it was guy-like of him but he wanted to have fun in his life. Albeit, with Vidisha next to him, but when push came to shove, he really had no clue as to what he would do.

On that last thought, Varun gave himself a mental smack down. Shit, maybe he really was over- reacting or had a spat with her mom. There was no need for him to jump of the edge like that everything was surely alright.

With positive, optimistic thoughts in mind he called Vidisha. She picked up and her tone, while a little better, was still subdued. Varun waited for her to tell him what was going on with her. He was a patient guy.

His patience had started to wear thin, when after ten minutes, Vidisha was still rambling. His temper had started to rise and with a bite he interrupted her.

"What is it Vidisha, will you tell me?"

Her next words confirmed his worst fears.

"Asha *bua* got a marriage proposal for me today."

Varun felt like he had swallowed poison. His throat worked but no words came out. What could he say. What did he have to offer? The buzzing in his head was interrupted by Vidisha's cries.

"Varun? Varun? Say something!?"

The voice that came from him didn't sound like his at all.

"When did this happen?"

Vidisha was talking, but Varun was oblivious. He heard the words but could barely register them. He knew that this was just the start. One proposal would lead to another and she would go and meet those weird men one day. And he knew her family. They loved her. She loved them too. Varun had sometimes questioned to himself her love for him. Did she love him as much as she loved her family? Was it more or was it less? Would she choose him over her family? Could he ask her to?

In all this mess, Varun became clear over one specific thing. There was no way on Earth her was ever going to make things difficult for Vidisha. In a moment of clarity, he realised that the only way he could show his love for Vidisha was by letting her go.

His next words left like he was signing his own death sentence.

"I think we should break-up."

He heard her phone fall. He called out to her but she was unable to hear him. His heart broke when he heard her cry. It killed him to have caused her such pain. When he could no longer bear her grief, he tore the phone away from him. Never had he felt so helpless. What kind of man was he that he couldn't even hold on to his love? He looked at the phone in his hand, the faint echoes of Vidisha's cries still present. In a fit of rage, his anger with

Vidisha, himself and the entire world bubbling out to him, he threw his cell at the wall. It hit the wall so hard, it shattered into tiny pieces. Staring at the remnants of his phone, he felt his life to be as shattered. He was unaware of the tears that had pooled in his eyes. Sliding to the floor, he gave himself over his despair and let oblivion take over.

11

BROKEN JIGSAW

It took Vidisha 5 weeks, 3 days, 6 hours, 27 minutes to accept the fact that she had broken up with Varun. The first few days had passed in a blur of tears. Her parents had gone out of their minds trying to console her. They assumed that she was still upset about the previous day's events. No matter how many times Vidisha had explained that her current state had nothing to do with that.

It had taken Reva's intervention to stop what would have been a pathetic descent into depression. Like the whirlwind she was, she had stormed into Vidisha's room a week after the breakup. Vidisha didn't even question how Reva knew about it. Vidisha watched with a numbing detachment as Reva went about airing the room. It was only when she turned on to her that Vidisha protested, and failed, miserably.

Reva forced Vidisha to get us and literally pushed her into the bathroom for a bath. While Vidisha was doing so Reva turned the Den of despair into Vidisha's cheery sanctuary.

For the first time in over a week, Vidisha felt like a human being. The pain and grief over losing Varun was still there. But she could feel a little bit of herself too, raring to fight.

As the weeks went by, everyday became a struggle. Even putting each foot forward became a chore. But somehow, Vidisha strived. She called and texted Varun but he was royally ignoring her. Each time he did so felt like fresh blow at her already bruised heart.

At times she wondered if he was the same man. Things had really changed for them. Varun had always been a head strong person and had immense control over himself and his feelings. Things were not easy on his part as well but he thought if this is what is needed to keep this girl happy be it. He knew initially things would be a little difficult but gradually they will all be too tough for them. She had no idea about his intent behind their breakup.

Varun understood he had to let her go. Being the strong one was necessary but it also sucked. His awareness of Vidisha's love cut at him, but he gritted himself against the pain.

At times, Vidisha texted Varun wanting to meet him but every time she did, Varun would have some excuse, refusing her. It was making her furious. She had thought it would be a matter of time before they got back. But she could see that things were getting dirty here.

One night she called him up at 1a.m & he picked up her call. His tone was distant and cold. Vidisha was unable to bear it anymore and she shouted out at him.

"What the hell is wrong with you? Why are you doing this? I am not living like this Varun."

She implored. It's been 15 days since we met.

"It's going to be like this Vidisha, it will be better for you if you understand this."

"What has got into you Varun?" Vidisha started to cry over the phone. She could not help herself.

Varun, who had never been able to see her tears, was for the first time quiet.

Something died in Vidisha then. She somehow dried her tears and silently hung up.

Time passed, Vidisha kept calling, kept texting. The calls became less, the texts became few. Vidisha understood the loss of that sparkle, but she kept on with her efforts. She was aware of Varun's love and his hurt. That was what urged her to keep making that effort.

Some 2 months later Vidisha was texting Varun, when he suddenly stopped to reply. He was reading the texts but not replying. That did such weird things to her. She lost count of the time she tried to sort out things with him. His replies had started to become so curt and clipped, it almost killed her.

One day, Vidisha lost it, she kept on calling him. She could just not handle all this shit.

Varun took the call but talked to her with no interest at all. This really upset Vidisha and she showed it. Seeing her grief Varun who had somehow barely managed to hold onto his on grief, also broke down. "Vidisha please don't make it so difficult for me. I love you that I can't do this to you. I cannot spoil your life. Please understand. I will need to hang up. Bye."

This went on for quite some time. It was 6–8 months that she dealt with a completely different side of Varun. Her anger had burned out and now she tried to understand things from his perspective.

She met him in a club after few weeks and they saw each other. He kept looking at her till he could, she kept looking at him. They did not say a word and crossed each other.

That night Vidisha texted Varun, "your eyes speak a lot and they say what you don't want to. Keep a check on them."

Varun replied with a Smiley.

The beautiful thing that was there in their relationship had gone. The more perfect they thought it was the more flawed it turned to be. Vidisha always boosted about how beautiful and liberating her relationship was. After this she was always regretting her pride.

The pain that Vidisha had felt initially had now dulled to a blunt ache. The thoughts and memories which had haunted her every second now came in fits and starts. Earlier, everything around her reminded her of Varun. She had disposed of already bruised heart.

So many memorabilia. Small things like cards and chocolates. But she couldn't part with the letters and notes they had exchanged over the years.

She put those, along with the charm bracelet that he had given her when he first proposed inside and old box and put it in the darkest corner of her closet where she wouldn't be assaulted by all those memories. Her heart had broken all over again, when she removed the bracelet, which had been an essential part of her for all these years. She had taken to wearing an old shirt of Varun's while sleeping. That was the closest she felt to him in months. Every night, she inhaled his scent before drifting off.

One day, Vidisha broke out of the melancholy that she had surrounded herself with. What triggered this was the result of her design course. Her first few assignments which had exceptionally good scored were marred by the last few scores which were pathetic.

For the first time ever, Vidisha was mad at herself. She took a close look at her life and where it was heading to. Yes, she was distressed and unhappy. But that was no excuse to deteriorate. She realised that these last months had affected her in more ways than one. Guilt swamped her. The disappointment and sadness of her parents were more effective than a bucket of ice water.

Maybe, just maybe, it was time she tried to start getting over Varun. It was time she stopped mourning.

The next few days, Vidisha immersed herself in improving her grades. She still had one finale to work on and she threw herself, heart and soul, into that. All her pent-up emotions, her grief, anger, loss, restlessness, she threw in her work.

Her hard work paid off and Vidisha salvaged her final grade. Once she graduated, Vidisha was at a loss. She had received a few offers from fashion companies in Delhi and Bombay. But there was a grain of dissatisfaction embedded in her.

She wanted to escape from the confines of Ranchi, no India itself. One evening, she was scrolling the net and she found herself on the web site of the University of New York. She browsed through its design programs and found herself intrigued. Hmm, it was a mere one year course. She could apply for it. Where was the harm in that? The next few days were spent in a flurry of references, collecting all required documents, proof reading statements of purpose and all. She did not tell her parents. She was aware of their worry and she hoped this new focus would ease their worries.

Finally, four days later, Vidisha mailed over her transcript to NYU and now came the worst part, waiting.

As she eased in her chair, she mused that this must have been how Varun felt when he was waiting for her reply. No! She was NOT thinking about that!

She got up and went down to lie on her bed. The way she was feeling, a year in America looked like exactly what she needed right now. She crossed her fingers and prayed with everything she had that she might be just that one step closer to the America Dream.

12

CARPE DIEM

When you work hard for something and you achieve it, the joy that goes through you is unparalleled. But when you achieve something big, when you are least expecting it, that sense of pride and satisfaction is even greater.

The day Vidisha received a reply from the enrolment offices at NYU, she was soaking in the sun and enjoying her morning coffee. She was in a state of semi- drowsiness and was feeling too lazy and cosy to even reach for her cell. Resigned, she raised her cup to take another sip of her personal ambrosia and picked up her phone. There was a new email notification. Seeing that it was from NYU Vidisha braced herself to be rejected and took a few fortifying gulps of coffee to steady her nerves.

Her next response could not have been predicted even by her, she sprayed out the entire coffee that was in her mouth all over herself. It ran down the front of her clothes and a few drops also landed on her phone. The mug she was holding in her hand had also jerked and now her hand had been scalded by hot coffee.

But Vidisha was unaware of all that. She started screaming at the top of her voice. Her mom had come running on hearing her shout.

"I GOT IN! I GOT IN!"

She gripped her mom and jumped like a crazy person. For the first time in ages, something went right for her.

She hugged her mother and was surprised to feel tears flowing down her cheeks.

Vidisha's parents were a conflicting mixture of pride, shock, anger and joy. When she explained how she applied to NYU, their faces were rounded in shock. When had their daughter become so big that she was ready to move halfway across the world without even telling them?

At first Vidisha's dad was adamant about not letting her go. How could he bear to part away from his beloved daughter? Who would, make his tea for him and pick out the perfect tie for his suit.

Vidisha's mom too was feeling an acute pain. Vidisha going away would be like losing a limb. But she was also fiercely proud of her child's independence. She had suspected for long time the relationship between Vidisha and Varun – her daughter may have been discrete but Madhavi was no fool. It was also obvious that the reason that Vidisha had almost become a zombie also had something to do with him. It had broken Madhavi's heart everyday on seeing her daughter in pain and she was helpless to do anything about it. It was only in the past month that she had begun to see a spark in Vidisha again. As her mother, Madhavi would make sure her daughter got the best of what she deserved. Convincing her husband would be a piece of cake.

Vidisha was overjoyed when her parents informed her that she could go to NYU. She felt like life was worth living again. Weeks passed in blur as she applied for her visa, shopped for necessities and getting her papers in order. If all went well she would be on a flight to New York in two months.

When Vidisha broke out the news to Reva and Saket, they both asked her the same question. A question she had been dreading.

"Did you tell Varun?"

Vidisha was confused. It had been months since had talked to Varun. The last few times she had attempted to talk to him he had either been aloof and distant and cold, or had ignored her completely.

How he would react to her going away. She had no idea. She wasn't even sure if he would miss her or would be relieved to escape her. But still, there was no harm in talking to him.

One night, she was sitting on her bed, her thumb hovering Varun's name. To call or not to call? - that was the question. It was merely a quarter after 11. He would be awake right now. Closing her eyes, she could reject it. The call connected and after two whole rings when no one picked up a lump settled in Vidisha's stomach. She refused to give into the tears that were pursuing behind her lids. Refused to show that was affected by his negligence. She refused to believe that their love was so weak that it could be broken by a mere thing like distance. In her heart of hearts, she hoped that they would be able to put behind them all their issues and get back together.

Crossing her fingers, she dialled his number once again. And again. And again. That night Vidisha fell asleep with sobs still wracking her body.

Meanwhile, in Mumbai, Varun ignored that last buzz of his cell phone. He'd known who was calling. He had been waiting for this call for weeks, the moment he had known. But now he couldn't bring himself to pick it up, knowingly it would be a final goodbye.

He was just not prepared to accept that Vidisha would be separated from him by continents.

These past months had been hell on Varun. His efforts to dig her out of his life were fucking useless. The desire to be with her had seeped down to his bones and every part of him ached to be with her. His mechanical resolve was the only thing that had him going.

He talked to Reva and Saket occasionally. Reva was still pissed off at him but it was Saket who had let slip Vidhi's move to the US. He had wanted to immediately come to Ranchi and prevent her from going. He had almost booked the ticket when the sane and rational part of his mind – the one he hated – stopped him. How could he stop her? The only reason he had given for the break had been that he didn't want to be on impediment to her happiness.

With a heavy heart, Varun steeled himself to not pick up the damn phone and tell her to stay. He let the despair roll over him and allowed him to be swallowed by the darkness.

Vidisha was spending as much quality time with friends and family as she could. She didn't even know when time flew by. Soon, it was time to leave. The night before, she sat with family for hours. Her parents, her brother and herself. They were enjoying the evening on their terrace. She was teasing her brother and trying to make him laugh. It was obvious that despite his teasing don't – care attitude, he was upset.

She had made what she was best at, coffee for everybody. She was sitting on the floor while he mom was oiling her hair. Vidisha revealed in the massage knowing it would be a long time before she would experience it again. Her dad didn't say much but his quite assuring smiles and gentle hugs spoke volumes. The Agarwal family stayed well up in the night. For the first time, her brother had got her a sexy watch from fossil and leather backpack that was cute in a BOHEMIAN CHIC kind of way. Her mom had already given her a bunch load of clothes and accessories but her real gift was the 50K that

Vidisha knew had come from the her savings. Her mom had told her to enjoy with that cash but she knew there was no way she was blowing up her mom's hard earned money on booze and dance. She looked suspiciously at her father. He was the only one who hadn't given her anything but her dad loved to pamper her with small things he thought she would like. That he hadn't made Vidisha's heart twinge a little.

Finally at around 3:00 AM, they threw up their flags and surrendered. Her brother had long given up and was fast asleep on the swing. And as if they couldn't even bear to be apart from her, Vidisha's parents went with her to her room.

The cornucopia of goodies laid out on her bed took her by surprise and her eyes filled fast with tears. There was a huge pile of all her favourite chocolates, a gorgeous, gorgeous pair of tan Converse high- tops. A pile of books, a new iPod and a shiny new tablet rounded off the haul. When she managed to tear away her eyes from the treasure trove on her bed, she saw her entire room had been decorated in balloons and ribbons. She knew, just knew who had done this. Her tears half-binding her, she swirled to hug her dad.

"I'll miss you so much, papa!" he sobs choked her throat.

"I'll miss you too beta." His voice was as heavy and his hug full of security and comfort.

That night, Vidisha slept tucked between her parents, something she hadn't done since the age of nine.

The next morning, her entire house was in shambles. Like a typical Indian mother, Madhavi had made all of Vidisha's favourite dishes and was trying to force-feed her all of it. When after the third gulab-jamun she could take no more, Vidisha put down her foot.

Vidisha had an 11:00AM flight to Bangalore and then she would be boarding for the US. Sukhmani and her brother had skipped school to see her off. Vidisha was in such a state of bliss that even her brother's grumbles were welcome.

She waited impatiently as her mom applied tika. She touched her parents feet and in a flurry of goodbyes was off on a new adventure.

13

EMPIRE STATE OF MIND

"The temperature outside......"

Vidisha woke up with a jolt. New York! She was finally there. Departing, customs and immigrations felt like a breeze. When she stepped out of the airport, she took a moment to inhale the essence of New York. Granted it mostly consisted of smoke but still, she was in NEW YORK! The city that never sleeps!

This was her first time abroad and no matter how cheesy it seemed, she was going to do all sorts of touristy New York thins. Exploring times square, Sotto, the met, and if possible, even Liberty Island.

But first things first, she hailed a cab which would take he to the apartment she would be living in. She would be rooming with two other girls, Dephne, a 23 year science major who was applying for research work and 18 year old Mikacla, a shy freshman who was studying law. Vidisha had thorough researched the apartment before agreeing to shack up. She and her parents had made a number of video calls and she felt as if she knew the girls for ages.

The next few days were spent in adjusting to living alone in a strange, new city. The foods, the atmosphere, the people, were a world apart from that homely Ranchi. It had taken a few tries but she was now familiar with taking the subway to college.

College was a brand new experience for her. Classes were nothing like back home. For one, there were a lot more guys studying fashion, most of who were gay. Plus, it was exciting to come to class where teachers were wearing shorter skirts than you.

Vidisha remembered that first day she had to go to college. Her class was to begin at 10:00 AM. So, Vidisha got up all bright and early. She took special care in making sure she looked good choosing formal dark chocolate trousers with a navy blue top. She put on a matching chocolate brown blazer and contrasted the whole look with a canary yellow tote bag. She looked at her watch. Great! it was only 8:15. What would she do the next hour and half?

Gradually, Vidisha settled into a routine. Home, college, home, college. She had made a bunch of new friends now but most of her time was spent in college.

Apart from her course, the only co-curricular activity she indulged in was the debate society. She had already participated in a few and was way over the moon when she won, not once, but twice.

In two months Vidisha was context with her life. She missed her parents, her brother, Reva, Saket and even Varun, but she was grateful for this experience.

One Saturday morning, Vidisha was sleeping in, taking complete advantage of a much needed break, when her phone rang. She let it go for the first time but when it rang again Vidisha picked it up to give the moron piece of her mind. Nobody fucked with her Saturday off.

"Hello?" she literally growled into her cell.

"Yeah. Hi. May i speak to Ms. Vidisha Agarwal please?" the voice was the rich baritone of a guy and definitely Asian. Vidisha forced herself to wake up. The crisp direct tone of the guy meant serious business.

"Yes. This is Vidisha. May i know who is calling?"

"Hi Vidisha. Good Morning. I hope i didn't get you at a bad time. By the way, my name is Dhruv Kapoor. I am a senior in the programming department. There was something i wanted to talk to you about if you are interested?"

Intrigued, Vidisha replied 'continue, I'm listening.'

"Brilliant! So, i am a member of young Indians on campus, an Indian community based society club and i happened to see your performance last week in the debate society and I would like to applaud your confidence and delivery of words.'

Vidisha gave a huge mental hurrah over this. It felt great to be appreciated.

"So, i would like to invite you to our club and see if you would be interested in applying for a membership. We realize how hard it is for immigrant students to be away from home and we try to bring as much off India as we can in their lives.

Vidisha's throat clogged at Dhruv's sensitivity. Before this she never really considered the worth and value of being an Indian. For the first time she missed her country.

"Dhruv, i would love to join the club. Tell me when and where, and I'll be there."

She jotted down the details and in a few days was a proud, card carrying member of young Indians on campus. There were around 15 members and Vidisha had made friends with all of them.

Because of her command over the language, Vidisha was used to writing speeches or articles or practising for all sorts of literary events. Dhruv was equally good and the two had become really close. She felt a certain connection towards him despite everything.

They met often for coffee and discussed pretty much everything under the sun. Despite being a computer geek, Dhruv made an effort to upturn the cliché. He was tall and lean and had an unhealthy obsession with his glasses. His friends swore that he had a new frame for every single day.

As the spring session was coming to an end Vidisha found herself with loads of free time. At first she was overjoyed. She spent her days exploring the city absorbing its vibrancy. But some days, when it was not possible to leave, Vidisha was bored out of her mind. She tried killing time by watching drama or experimenting with food but was still filing restless. She was fiddling with her laptop when she absently opened a new word document. Just for the heck of it. Vidisha typed a few lines on her experience in NY till now. She poured out her emotions, the good, the bad and the ugly, into her writing. Around two hours later, Vidisha felt purged and found a new hobby for herself.

Since then, Vidisha made a point to write a few articles every few days. Mostly she wrote about her feelings. Those things she was unable to tell others. She wrote about books, fashion, movies, love, and loss anything which caught her fancy. On a particular bad day she wrote about Varun, the good times and the bad. She wrote about their love and above all, she wrote about hope. She was out with Dhruv one day when she received a call from Daphne. "Hey babes ! Where are you ?" "Hi Daph. I'm out with Dhruv right now. Oh, and I'll be crossing Starbucks. Want me to get you evening java?"

"Yeah love, my usual. Listen, my laptop's broken down and I really need to send some important mails. Can I borrow yours? "

"Of course, babe. You really don't have to ask. It's on my desk. See you in some time. "

"Thanks babe. You're a complete life saver. Muah. Bye." As Vidisha was hanging up, she remembered he laptop was in sleep mode and her articles had been open. Eh, whatever Daphne would manage it.

An hour later when she reached home, Daphne and Mikaela both jumped on her, squealing like little girls instead of nature women. And both were speaking at once.

"Oh my god! You are so good!" "Why didn't you tell us?" "I want more! I want more!" "Dude you have to forward me the link I was only able to read a handful."

Vidisha managed to untangle herself from her friends and took in a huge gulp of air.

"What on earth are you guys talking about? I swear it's like you're speaking Latin."

"Vidz, we're talking about your blogs. Don't act like you don't know!"

"Okay. Guys, I'm really lost here. Help me out a bit?"

Then Daphne explained how she had opened Vidisha's laptop and seeing the article first thing, she hadn't been able to help herself from reading the first few lines and once she started, she was unable to stop herself.- Daphne's Expression became apologetic to her. After finishing one she opened the other and read them and when Mikaela came in she made her read it too, and now both of them were crazy on love with Vidisha's writing. Daphne loved one on friendship while Mikaela was almost starry - eyes over the one on Indian society.

When Vidisha explained that those were not blogs, both girls had an incredulous questioning look on their faces.

"Why in sweet name of God, it's not?" Exclaimed Daphne.

"Umm, because I never thought of it that way."

Mikaela piped in, "you really should Vidz, it's really cool. Why don't you start now? We'll help!

Vidisha was in a huge bubble of excitement. Daphne was a pro at stuff like this. They chose backgrounds and named it "A Slice of life" But the next morning her blog was up and running and the first part she posted was her write up on friendship titled "The Bookworm, the Maniac and the Romantic." It was a slice of life in her antics with Reva and Saket.

Initially Vidisha was unsure about posting so much about her private life online, but gradually she received an enthusiastic response. Not only, had many of her classmates, friends and family read it, but even her professors.

It had been a week ago when one of her professors mentioned that she read the blog and she liked it a lot.

Vidisha was so ecstatic that she began to work even harder on the blog.

Among her Indian friends Dhruv was ultra-excited over her work and always lent a encouraging hand to Vidisha.

Though far, far away from home Vidisha was beginning to feel at home.

14

THE DAM BREAKS!!

One Father's day, Vidisha's mood was spectacularly morose. She had talked to her dad for an hour or so on Skype but was still feeling melancholic.

She sat down in front of her laptop and began to type. She wrote about her father, his goodness and his warmth. She wrote of his booming laugh. But most of all she wrote about the security and love he provided to the family. For Vidisha, her dad was her rock who protected her from every nightmare. She names that post 'Love you, Dad!"

A few weeks later, there was a party at Dhruv's apartment. Most of the YIOC members were present as well as a number of other people. Vidisha hadn't wanted to go but Dhruv had insisted. That day happened to be the 4th year anniversary of her and Varun being together and somehow Vidisha was missing him all the more. You know something, about absence making the heart grow fonder.

They barely exchanged texts and communications was at an all-time low. Sometimes, Vidisha had to literally force him to talk. OK occasions, when she made stupid jokes or acted a little crazy, she could feel him fighting a laugh. The fact that she could still affect him touched Vidisha's heart.

So, when she received no acknowledgment from him that day, she was pretty much down in the dumps. Her mood had grown steadily worse and she just wanted to crawl in bed with a pint of ice - cream and the latest season of Game of Thrones.

When Dhruv insisted on her coming, she tried like hell to get out of it but he wouldn't take no for an answer. So, Vidisha forced herself to dress like a presentable human being and had to act like a social, friendly person.

At the party, Vidisha made a large vodka tonic for herself and made her way quietly to the balcony and sat down on the floor, hoping she wouldn't draw anyone's attention. Her thoughts were muddled and she was staring absently into her glass.

"You still love him, don't you?"

Vidisha gave a startled look and frowned when she saw Dhruv starring.

"I don't know what you're saying" Vidisha closed her eyes and leaned on the railings, hoping Dhruv would take the hint and leave. But, apparently it really wasn't her day.

"If you love him so much, why are you guys not together?"

Vidisha's head came up with a snap and she was sure her eyes reflected her anger.

"You know, that is really, really none of your business."

"Maybe, but we're really good friends Vidisha and I don't care if it is or not my business. Not many people I can say that about. But I am really going to do all that it takes to make you happy, even your anger."

Seeing that Dhruv intended to plant himself next to her, she gave a resigned sigh.

'Fine, Yes! I still love him. Always have and will probably always do. No matter how hard, I try; I can't seem to get him out of me. It's like, he's in every part of me, my soul, my skin, my blood, he's there and I can't help It.!"

This last part ended in a scream and there was a debate on who was more shocked, Vidisha or Dhruv.

"Ha! I knew it! You were hiding some pretty big secrets. Now come on. Give me details. 'And Vidisha,' - his tone was utterly serious now - ' you can really trust me.

And maybe it was the alcohol or maybe she had been bottling too much inside of her. Vidisha broke down and spilled her innermost fears and desires to a stranger with who she felt a keen sense of kinship.

Dhruv turned out to be a perfect gentleman. He listened attentively. Made all the right sounds at all the right part and even age her handkerchief when tears spilled down her cheeks.

After Vidisha had calmed down a bit, she gave Dhruv a thankful smile. She may have not known it bit this catharsis had long been due.

"It's okay to fight your love, for your love Vidz."

Vidisha looked at him.

I'm not taking his side, but I kind of get him. Partly because I would have done the same thing probably. He thought he was allowing you spread your wings. What he didn't realise was that he is your wings. Don't blame him for that. You have been apart for more than a year. Neither of you are the people who you were then. When you go back in a few months why don't you try again? Maybe you'll get a different answer this time. "

Vidisha starred at Dhruv in shock. Of all things, she had not expected this insight and wisdom from a guy. Touched at his concern, Vidisha thought, that no matter what else she would take from America, a true, lifelong Friend would definitely be one of them.

Vidisha was in a shaking quivering mess. Why, why had she left herself been dragged into this quagmire? It had all begun a month ago. She was doing well in college, her blog gaining more, popularity and followers each day. Yeah life was good.

So how had she managed to fuck up in this way?

While Vidisha was completely fine with participating in debates and extempore and small scales like in the class or between clubs, she was so not okay with competing against not one, but two Ivy league institutions on a very, very large scale. Columbia and Harvard were only really amateurs.

She still hadn't found out who had put down her name for the literary events, but when she did, heaven help that person.

Granted, she was not the only person participating - it was open for all - but a lot of people were naming on her. Dhruv and the rest of the YIOC's was her cheer gang. Every day, they barged in her house made her practise mock drills until she almost went out of her mind. Half the times, she had to literally push them forcibly out of her house.

She had been cramming quotes, theories, famous philosophers of famous thinkers and what - not for days. She could now recant literary trivia in her sleep and in good things; her vocabulary had increased in leaps and bounds.

The literary festival was to cover four days ending on Sunday, with a get together for faculty, participants and winners. It would consist of cocktail and dinner.

The dress code was black and Vidisha was grated up and excited to attend it.

So, it was the D-day and with a grand flourish the events began. Vidisha participated in poetry, writing, recitation and calligraphy. As a design student calligraphy was a breeze for her and at the end of the day she even won second prize in it. Vidisha was ecstatic! The competition for creative writing was also fierce and this was one event where she and to preserve her reputation. Thanks to her special effort to her selection of words. Her efforts bore fruit when she was announced as the 1st position holder.

The best two days passed without much excitement. Vidisha just won a measly consolation prize in an essay competition. She now focused all her energy in the debate and extempore. She brushed up her current affairs knowledge and went to bed taking two lozenges to keep her throat clear.

She woke up bright and early and carefully selected her clothes. Her first event was her debate and she was specially prepared for it. Because of its popularity, the debate was being held in Caspery the campus auditoriums. Vidisha didn't even dare look at the crowd she would definitely like her nerve. Instead she focused on her opponent and his tirade. He was from Yale and an eloquent speaker. But his appeal had a few flaws which, like a starving predator, Vidisha pounced upon and ripped to pieces. Unsurprisingly, she was one of the three finalists who would make it to the final ever extempore.

The extempore round would take place two hours later after lunch and the topic would be given on the spot. Vidisha was battling butterflies the size of dinosaur's and could barely manage to choke down her meal.

Dhruv was pounding her shoulders in an effort to calm her down. She received a pleasant surprise in the form of Daphne and Mikaela, who, as it turned out had been there in the audience for her debate. Mikaela had been recorded Vidisha's performance and was now showing it to her. They planned to stay through the entire event and Daphne, the life- saving goddess that she was, had arranged for a kick- ass dress for Vidisha to wear that night.

When, it was time, Vidisha was waiting backstage, all alone, for her turn. It had been then that she has started hyperventilating. As she began cursing the person who has signed her up, she recalled that she herself had lit down her name on excitement. Well, now she has no one to blame but herself. She was number 2 on the list and the previous speaker was just winding up her points. Her judges, in an attempt to raise the level of the speakers, had announced that the topics would be more subjective then objective. Shit, this meant that the topics would be more of a personal and emotional nature rather than one that could be spoken about rationally or with a cool head.

Crossing her fingers and praying that she would get a safe, easy topic, Vidisha walked onto the stage. She heard a great encouraging shouts and cheers which she assumed were here friends. On a podium on a side were five envelopes fanned out. They contained the topics for the extempore. A hush had fallen over the auditorium. She picked up the first envelope she touched and pulled out the card.

Karma truly is a bitch. She smiled at the irony of her situation. Walking over to the microphone she spoke -

"Good afternoon, ladies and gentlemen. My name is Vidisha Agarwal and I shall be speaking on the topic - 'Love is everlasting'."

15

A BALLET OF LIGHTS

When you observe it clearly, a year does not even seem like much time. Days fly into weeks and weeks into months. And yet sometimes, a single moment stretches out for what feels like eons.

What Vidisha was feeling right now was the former. Really! Where had the time gone? It felt like yesterday when she boarded the flight for New York. And now, it was time for her to leave. In around a month and half, her course would be over and soon Vidisha would be leaving behind an entire life. Her last days were spent going to all those places that were absolutely necessary to visit. She went to Times Square with Dhruv and a few friends from college. They danced on the streets experimented with all sorts of food and had a major blast. They had gotten dead drunk. And Dhruv, who was US born and bred, burst into an ear bleeding rendition of some Arijit Singh's song. Ray, another guy in their group had to calm his hand in his mouth to shut him up. Vidisha and her friends Megan and Trish were giggling like crazy. The group was doing shots in some pub in Greenwich Village. They had got a farewell gift for Vidisha. Unfortunately, dead- drunken Vidisha teared up and was now bawling like a seven - year old at the top of her voice. Even all the people giving them the evil eye did not deter her.

"Oh! I love you guys so much. I'm going to take you with me. I'll smuggle you in my bag and when we clear customs and go home I'll ask my parents to adopt you." Vidisha said to the group, completely drunk. They were now at Ray's apartment.

Megan, equally wasted, replied - "But I won't be able to fit in your grey case. Trish might but I want to go in your black case."

They had a serious discussion on the benefits of travelling in a suitcase and one by one they all crashed off to sleep.

Clothes. Clothes everywhere. It seemed as if Vidisha would drown under the flood of clothes that had piled up her bedroom. When had she been bought half the stuff?

"Daphne! Mikky! Help me!" "Oh god! Do you have to be a drama queen?" Daphne's voice came through the adjoining wall.

Vidisha had a serious problem in her hands. In New York, she never had to think twice about what she was wearing and had acquired a collection of clothes that could barely be worm in Mumbai, let alone Ranchi.

She had separated those clothes which she absolutely could not take back. She choked her hands on some of the pieces. Too bad it happened just at the moment Daphne and Mikaela entered the room.

"Dude, you have a way too unhealthy obsession with your clothes."

"Oh, shut up! What do you know about the sacrifice I'm making - Vidisha mock-sniffer - "Anyways, as you know, once I go back I cannot wear most of these clothes. Somehow, wearing a neon boon tube with super-ripped shorts in the street is frowned upon in India. And, because I am so generous, and merciful, I am requesting all of my pretty babies to you guys. Treat them well. Vidisha broke off on another sob.

Finally the day came when she had to say goodbye forever. Dhruv, Daphne and Mikaela came to see her off at the airport. She hugged Daphne and Mikaela and whispered to them - "Don't become strangers, you guys!"

"We'll miss you Vidz. Damn we're going to miss you!" - Daphne and Mikaela wiped tears of their own.

She now turned to Dhruv, with whom she always felt at home. She hugged him tightly too.

"Thanks Dhruv, thanks for everything".

"No problem, Vidz. Go safely. Call me once you're home and keep in mind what I told you."

With a brush of his lips on her forehead, he let go of the girl whose friendship he had come to treasure.

With a final wave, Vidisha went through the gates and said goodbye to a special part of her life.

Vidisha woke up with a start. In two hours she would be landing in Mumbai and she would be staying there for the weekend. Reva had moved to Mumbai around six months back and was now working at an IT firm. She has talked to her parents and told them she would be taking a small break with Reva and then coming back. She refused to think of the other person who lived in Mumbai. She wondered if she would get to meet him. At the airport, she was picked up by Reva who greeted her with a scream loud enough to shatter windows.

"I missed you so much, Vidhi!"

Vidisha too felt the same. She just was unable to formulate the words. The entire ride back home, both girls barely stopped talking. They had a year's quota of gossip/news to update. Calls, texts and skyping were no match to actually having a face to face conversation with a real person.

Reva mentioned that Vidisha's blogs were a huge hit with her friends and colleagues.

"… I especially liked that last one which has the link to the video of yours of the extempore. It made me want to believe in love, it was that good."

Actually, it has been Mikaela who had attached that to the video at the last moment, something about visually connecting to her followers. It had received a good response. Unconsciously, she wondered if Varun had seen it.

It took her to her rid of all the jet - lag and then she was ready to party. The night she arrived, she was too tired to anything. So, Vidisha and Reva stayed up till late in the night.

At they were taking about her life in New York, Reva quietly asked. - "Have to talk to Varun yet?"

"No" she whispered. She desperately wanted to meet him. She had hoped she would, but how would it be possible.

She tried to ignore the pain and changed the topic. Reva, however, silenced her with her next question.

"Do you want me to tell him?" Desperately wanting to say yes, Vidisha portrayed an aloof demeanour and waved off Reva's offer.

"Chuck it, babe. I'm hungry. Let's make Maggie. It's been a year since I've had it. "Come on." She dragged Reva to the kitchen successfully changing the topic. Or so she thought.

When Vidisha was sleeping off the final few stages of jet-lag, Reva was going some serious scheming.

She was at her office because she didn't want Vidisha to overhear her. Poor Vidisha! She was so transparent. Reva could see how Vidisha struggled with herself. Well, she was going to do her friend a favour and take the decision out of her hands.

She called the one person who could solve the dilemma.

"Hello?" "Hey stranger, longtime no see?" "What do you want Reva?" "Informing you that we have a dinner date tonight." "When did that happen?" Exclaimed Varun. "Now, right now!"

There was definitely something fishy going on. Vidisha could scent it in the air. Reva had planned a major girl's night out and had told Vidisha to dress up super - sexy.

Vidisha had chosen a white bandage dress that hugged very curve of her body. This she teamed up with bright coral puckers and coral pumps. Diamond studs and a coral accented clutch completed her look.

Satisfied with the results, Vidisha waited for Reva to get dressed. There was something going on with that girl. She had been behaving so weirdly the entire day.

Finally, Reva came out, dressed in hot leather skirt, black tank and knee length boots. Only Reva could have pulled off this look.

They were going to "He said, she said" a popular spot in Mumbai. Because it was a Friday evening there was a bit of a crowd gathered.

They entered the club and they made their way to the bar. Reva ordered a Bloody Mary and Vidisha her usual G&T. They were sitting, sipping their drinks when a warm baritone washed over her and lit her up.

"May I join you ladies?"

Vidisha looked up to see Varun standing, looking as handsome as the last time she saw him.

Varun had burst into goose bumps when Reva told him, to come over. There could only be one reason and one reason only - Vidisha.

He took the time and address and promised he would be there. Over time, he realised he missed Vidisha more than he needed her to be free. Realising that he would have a lot of grovelling to do, he garnered some extra ammunition. Some roses and chocolates would do the trick. He felt full of life after a long, long time.

Maybe, he would walk out of this & with his heart restored.

Vidisha realised that she was not breathing and her mouth was hanging open. Reva punched her to jolt her kit of her reveries.

Her heart was pounding on her chest and the ache in her heart intensified and eased all at the same time.

"What…? How…? When…?? She looked at Reva who was looking disgustingly proud at herself. Catching Vidisha's glare, she managed to contour her face in an expression of innocence.

"What? I thought it would be nice to catch up with old friends."

Before Vidisha could say anything else Varun had engulfed her in a bone - crunching hug. Surprised, she returned it and mused at how normal he was behaving.

"Hi, how are you?" - he whispered into her ear.

"I'm good, you?" - She took the opportunity to breathe in his comforting scent. Deciding not to drudge out the past and live in the moment, the three friends got down to party. She gave Varun a pointed look which he chose to ignore as he lit up his cigarette and she ignored his raised eyebrows when she ordered a JD on the rocks for the next round.

In two hours, all three were pretty high. Sorting the check, they left and made plans to meet at a nearby coffee- shop. Another two hours later, after the buzz had worn off, they made plans to go on a drive. Vidisha had never felt so alive. They parked near a deserted stretch of road where she and Varun danced in the middle of the road. They had masala - chai and vada-pav from a road side vendor at 3'0clock in the morning. Exhausted they crashed at Reva's flat at around 4 AM and fell fast asleep.

They woke up at 12 noon and had a breakfast of eggs, toast and coffee. They dropped Varun at his place and planned to meet for a movie in an hour or so. They got ready and Reva & Vidisha reached the theatre before Varun. As they were waiting, Reva excused herself to take a call. After hanging up, she turned to Vidisha - "*Suno*, I've got to go to office for some urgent work. You guys go in. I'll join you in an hour or so."

Vidisha wanted to protest, but how could she? Work had to come before leisure. As they were talking, Varun came up to them bearing Nacho's and cold drink. Seeing Vidisha's expression she asked her, "wassup? Everything okay? "

They explained the situation to him. Even he did not object to Reva going. With a promise of coming back in an hour or so, Reva left them and they went in to watch the movie.

Vidisha was uber - aware of Varun sitting next to her. The envelope of darkness surrounding then heightened their senses. Her nerves were crackling. She needed Reva to act as a neutralizer. Somehow, she made it to the interval. Using the excuse of going to the washroom, she called up Reva.

"Hello?" "Reva, how much lo her will it take? The movie is halfway done. Come quick?? "Yeah. No, I won't be coming. Enjoy. Bubyeee." and she hung up.

Vidisha stared at her phone in astonishment. Furiously she called her back.

"Reva Narayan! You better have fucking good excuse as to why not."

"Vidhi, you're a smart girl. Can't you work it out?"

"Huh. I'm so not getting you."

"Oh god! You're so dense. Vidisha baby. I am NOT coming, as in Nada. What I am actually doing it being your best friend. Did you really think I was going to act as a third wheel between you and Varun all day? Take the bull by hors, love and fell free. It's high time you two imbeciles put away your ego and think of each other for a change. Now go, enjoy the movie, go for Dinner, bang each other blind, I don't care. Just give me all the sexy details tomorrow.

And with a snigger that would do the devil proud she hung up. Vidisha could only stare at her cell in astonishment. It seemed as if Reva would never quit surprising her. Still in daze she walked back into the theatre and sat down on her seat.

"What took you so long? Varun enquired. Gazing at him, Vidisha decided to seize the moment. "No, it's nothing. Umm, tell me about you. How have you been doing these past years?"

In the end, they got thrown out of the hall creating a ruckus. Varun still blamed Vidisha for instigating the popcorn fight. Giggling like teenagers, they stood outside the theatre planning what to do. It was barely 1'0clock and neither of them hungry much. The weather itself was cool with barely a hint of sun.

On a spontaneous whim, they decided to go for a drive. All the while they were talking. By mutual consent, neither of them dredged up the past. They only cared for the moment. Both hearts, bruised and lonely, healed because of each other.

On the evening, they went to the beach and lost themselves in the crowd. When Varun held Vidisha's hand it felt as natural as breathing. When he steadied her to prevent her from tripping, Vidisha felt as if she was slipping in a comfortable old shirt.

As twilight faded into a star- lit night, neither of the two wanted the day to end. They made their way to Varun's flat where they ordered some food to be delivered. When the meal came, Vidisha was surprised to see Varun pouring two glasses of wine in a candlelit table. "Since when did you start drinking wine? "

Varun gave her a sheepish look. "Actually I once had to order a case for an office event and the dealer gave me an extra bottle as a sample. Before today, I never needed to use it."

Vidisha was touched at the gestures. Together, they got down to a simple meal of pasta and gnocchi, talking of everything and nothing, of love, life and loss of Varun and Vidisha. They had long since given their hearts and souls to each other so giving up their bodies was not difficult. The whisper of clothes in skin, of hushed laughs echoed throughout the house. Dinner was forgotten, the world was for forgotten, and reality was forgotten. Drenched in the warm blaze of candles,

Vidisha accepted Varun's kiss. With it she also accepted his unspoken apology.

The fire that burned around them blazed far stronger and far hotter in Varun's eye. They loosened the reins of their passions and let instinct take over. Finally, they reached the crescendo together and let themselves be taken over by peaceful oblivion.

Waking up in the morning to Varun's face had always been one of Vidisha's fantasies. To see it fulfilled flooded her with exhilaration. Last night bad been wondrous and she had absolutely no regrets. The only thing she hoped for was that Varun had none too. Although, swing the smile and twinkle with which he woke up and looked at her, regret was to be the last thing on his mind.

Maybe she suffered some sort of mental damage last night it her brain - to - mouth filters had stopped working, but she blurted out the first thing in her mind.

"What changed your mind?" She couldn't help it and now she waited with baited breath for his answer. Unable to meet his eyes, she heard hesighs before answered.

"Honestly, what actually gave me a jolt was that video of your extempore. Reva sent me the link and how could I not see it. That would mean missing an opportunity to be close to you. I had been living with much guilt since I let you go. Earlier I thought it was what was best, but for whom? By taking the decision out of your hands, the only person I was protecting was me. And God! Don't even get started on when you were going to the US. I was almost ready to stop you from going. I hated every single day of my life without you Vidisha Agarwal. Take away everything from me and I can survive, but you are my very soul, my reason to live, how could I survive without you?

Varun leaned over to kiss away her tears, tears that she didn't even know where there. Finally, she was at some peace. The dressed together in silence, but not an awkward one. Rather, it was comfortable and reflected an ease brought about by familiarity.

Reva was grinning like a proud mama bear when Vidisha and Varun attempted and failed! To sneak into her apartment. Vidisha kept on glaring at her and Varun had his usual sweet smile, loaded with healthy dose of embarrassment. He completely ignored Reva and went into her room to retrieve Vidisha's luggage. Vidisha ignored Reva's nudges and pleas for details. With a promise of later. In some time, the awkwardness dissolved into the camaraderie forged from years of genuine friendship and the three made their way to the airport. The impending departure was playing havoc with the lover's nerves. The entire ride, Varun didn't let go of Vidisha's hand.

At the airport, Reva said goodbye to her dearest friend. However good bye was not very distraught as Vidisha had shared with her some rather pleasant news this morning. Varun on the other hand, had a hard time letting her go. Reva had moved away a little to give them some privacy. He was hugging her close as he asked her - "We're Forever?"

Vidisha replied - "Darling, we were never over."

EPILOGUE

As Vidisha went to the airport to check in, she mulled over the piece of news she had kept from Varun. After almost two years of separation, it had been difficult for him to say goodbye to Vidisha knowing he had just got her back. But Vidisha had had a major surprise for him in around three months.

While applying for jobs, she had sent her resume to many fashion houses and had received many positive replies. One of them had been from Mumbai. They were a prestigious firm and had a specially carved niche for her kind of style.

Earlier she had been a little hesitant over accepting the Mumbai offer but after this weekend she would be saying a resounding 'Yes' to them. She had already talked to her parents and after some hard core pleading, begging and crying they had reluctantly said 'Yes'.

So, that meant in three months' time, she would be shifting to Mumbai, living with Reva and falling in love with her boyfriend all over again.

Vidisha happily went home, pleased with everything around her. Maybe, karma isn't such a bitch after all.

Love is Everlasting

Simple 4 letter words that can make you feel a million things.

It seems it has a life cycle of its own.

Taking that one step, a person goes on believing in forever and in promises of forever. Life becomes beautiful and that person becomes life itself. The one and the only. They say beauty lies in the eye of the beholder. So, who becomes more beautiful? The person who says that you're beautiful, or the object of appreciation? From your morning coffee to a long drive, there is only one person you want to share these experiences and memories with. The sensation of lingering lips and fingers remain with you for weeks after he holds you and kisses you. Even after spending the entire day with him, you fantasize about him the remaining time. You even feel like cherishing every single emoji and text he has ever sent you. Your schedule can be completely reorganised just to accommodate him. You walk up to the mirror just because he said "who would not fall for those eyes". He is the one who can bring out the inner girl of the most outspoken tomboy.

A few, more steps together. Even when separated by distance, you can be somewhat context if you talk to him. Mundane topics also acquire her sparkle of novelty. Daily 'I love you' and 'I miss you' become the norm and they never grow old. He becomes your best friend. After all, the trust connections are often based on genuine friendship. Every single memory becomes a treasure.

Often when, you're completely head over heels, you also name your imaginary babies and your imaginary fights start to become real. When the comfort zone warms off you start to hold your own. New questions are formed, such as 'you think you can talk to me like that?' What kind of attitude is this? Or 'Do you even love me anymore? That is when you start questioning your 'forever'. Life's like this, love's like this.

The journey of love is full of twists and turns. There comes a stage of possession where you think that 'she is mine' and so it's okay to tell her what to do, even to shout at her. This is when you enter the next phase of love. How does it happen that the person, whom you love, starts to take you for granted? And you don't even realize it! The romance diminished and familiarity bleeds into monotony. Soon, there are less drives, and less kisses - the ones that curl your toes - and even less 'oh my god' factors. Where does this spark go?

A time when you could not go a single day without meeting him, becomes 'ok, let's meet up this weekend, if I'm free.' It's just so bland.

The thunder storm which defined the zenith of your relationship has now become a weak drizzle. You drift away because of silly reasons. What was once a mighty oak has now become brittle? It crumbles so easily and all that you're left holding dust and ashes. When forced to face reality, even the strongest of bonds seem to dissolve like salt in water.

Yes, love means sacrifice. But does it mean the sacrifice of the one you love? Is it justified, to rip that love, you were given. To shred and trample all over it and they say 'It was because I love you'.

Separating from the person you love, in the name of love, correct? It's funny how staying together and staying apart acquire the same meaning.

Honestly, love is something so pure, that even if it is not given a definition or a tag, even if it is surrounded by distance & separation, it still prevails.

Pretending that you aren't, that you don't give a damn, even when it is eating you from the inside out, is not heroic. You're hurting no one but yourself.

So just follow your own mantra. If she's yours, she yours. No matter what. Period.

'If it has to happen, it will' is so yesterday. "If it has to happen, freaking make it happen today!"